# THE COMPOUNDING LIVES OF JAKOB

COLIN RAYMOND

Colin Raymond/The Compounding Lives of Jakob
Printed in the United States of America

The Compounding Lives of Jakob/ Colin Raymond -- 1st ed.

ISBN 9798837025402 Print Edition

# CONTENTS

Life 18.0 - Airport Northern Virginia 2021.................................1

Life 1.0 - Childhood Austria 1459 ...............................5

Life 18.0 - Northern Virginia 2021 ...............................9

Life 1.0 - The Emperor's Clothes Austria 1468..........................15

Life 18.0 - Time to Go Virginia 2021 ...............................21

Life 1.0 - Everyone Sins Austria 1469.............................27

Life 18.0 - Florida 2021 ...............................33

Life 1.0 - Investing Augsburg 1470 ...............................39

Life 18.0 - Searching the Net Florida 2021 ...............................43

Life 1.0 - Double Entry Italy 1473...............................51

Life 18.0 - Theories Florida 2021 ...............................57

Life 1.0 - Sibylle the Protestant Germany 1497 ...............................63

Life 18.0 - ICU Florida 2021 ...............................71

Life 1.0 - The Barmaid Augsburg 1499 ...............................75

Life 18.0 - Blackfeet Nation Montana 2021 ...............................81

Life 1.0 - Spoiled Children Hungary 1515 ...............................91

Life 18.0 - Sunset Montana 2021 ...............................101

Life 5.0 - Holland 1625 ...............................109

Life 18.0 - LA 2021 ...............................117

Life 18.0 - Leaving LA 2021 ...............................135

Life 10.0 - Red Shield 1769 ...............................137

Life 18.0 - Zurich 2021 ...............................145

Life 10.0 -Rothschild Phoenix 1769............................155

Life 18.0 - Augsburg 2021 .....................................159

Life 10.0 - Juden Frankfurt 1770 ...........................167

Life 18.0 - A Drive to France 2021 .........................171

Life 10.0 - Kindermacht Frankfurt 1770 .................177

Life 18.0 - Annecy France 2021 .............................185

Life 10.0 - Five Arrows Europe 1798.......................191

Life 18.0 - Chez Enfants 2021 ................................195

Life 13.0 - Hispaniola 1844 ...................................199

Life 18.0 - Plaka 2021 ...........................................203

Life 13.0 - Hispaniola 2 - 1844..............................211

Life 18.0 - Budapest 2021......................................215

Life 14.0 - Louisiana, USA 1864............................221

Life 18.0 - Sounding Board 2021 ...........................225

Life 16.0 - Girls' Education 1950............................229

Life 18.0 - Fade to Gray 2021 ................................235

Life 18.0 - Ding Dong 2021 ...................................243

A note on historical accuracy ................................245

*This book is dedicated to my own Kellyann.*

*Many thanks to my wife, father, mother, sister, sister-in-law, and daughters.*

*"Compound interest is the most powerful force in the universe."*

Attributed to Albert Einstein

Riquewihr, France 2009. Excerpt from a partially burned diary in German found during excavation to replace a municipal water pipe. Estimated date 1730. Riquewihr Bureau of Antiquities, folio 2009-145.

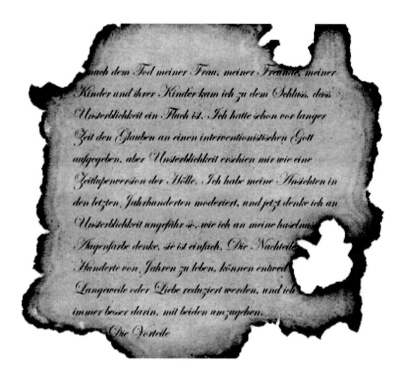

Translated from German.

*[Burned section] … Nevertheless, after the death of my wives, my friends, my children, and their children, I concluded that immortality was a curse. I had long ago given up believing in an interventionist God, but not dying after two centuries seemed like a slow-moving version of hell. Wealth made it only slightly more bearable. I have moderated my thoughts over the last several centuries, and now I think of immortality the same way I think about my eye color. It simply is. The drawbacks of living for hundreds of years can be [Burned section] to either boredom or love, and I am getting better at dealing with both. The benefits... [Burned section]*

# CHAPTER 1

# LIFE 18.0 - AIRPORT NORTHERN VIRGINIA 2021

J akob's flight landed with no problems. But problems quickly appeared as he walked through the baggage claim. Six airport cops, hands on their holsters, and two beefy men dressed in black, entered through a secure door and fanned out, scanning the crowd. Jakob glanced towards the bathrooms, but he'd have to walk across the open area to reach them. Instead, he casually ducked behind a row of luggage carts and pulled a wig and dress from his carry-on. Controlling his breathing, he pulled the thin, cotton, full-length beach dress over his head. This proved difficult because of the humidity that washed in as the doors to the outside opened. Then he pulled on the blonde wig and oversized sunglasses.

Digging around in his carry-on, he walked to the exit and got in the short line for cabs. Just another woman wearing men's shoes. A cab pulled up and Jakob jumped in, the driver's strong cologne wafting out of the open door. After telling the cab driver to head towards the Watergate, he slumped down. Peeking out the side window, he watched three cops and both mercenaries rush out and scan the oval of streets outside Reagan National airport.

One mercenary sprinted towards the departing line of cabs moving slowly toward the Parkway merge. Jakob could hear his heart beating as the sprinter got closer.

He prepared to open the door and run if the mercenary stopped the cab. But luck intervened, and the sprinter noticed that the cab behind Jakob's contained a blonde woman. Jakob watched as she spilled her coffee when the black-clad man pounded on the windshield and insisted, with his hand on his holster, that the cab pull over. Jakob stayed low and watched the cab driver emerge, screaming in Pashtun at the man in black, as Jakob's cab slid into traffic on the Parkway.

After a few seconds, he realized he'd been holding his breath. With a quiet intake of air, he handed a $50 bill to his driver and huskily said, "Sorry, plans changed. Please drop me off at 15th and Bell in Crystal City."

He'd have to walk two blocks to the Metro out in the open, but it would be easier to lose a tail once on the Metro. The fifty seemed to do the trick, as the driver dropped him off a minute later with no complaint.

After throwing away the glasses, wig, and dress, he matched the pace of others on the sidewalk and headed to the Metro entrance. He held a hand by his face to shield it from cameras and because his head was spinning with questions.

*How had they spotted me? They hadn't flagged me as I boarded, or they'd have picked me up at the gate. It must have been passport control at Reagan National or the airport's facial recognition systems. Either way, it sucks. Whoever is trying to capture me is with the government, or they've hacked into TSA's secure systems. To have mercenaries waiting at this airport implies they probably have them at others. They must have a nearly unlimited budget.*

The Metro gliding into the station interrupted his thoughts, and he climbed aboard. He didn't care where it went. He just had to put distance between himself and the airport. As he sat, he took his thin jacket off and inverted it. Two stops later, he put it back on inside out, exited and crossed the platform with his head down and a slight limp to throw off gait recognition software, and got on a different Metro.

*Whoever is after me either wants to extort me, or they want to find out why I'm not dead, even if it means killing me. They're well resourced, connected, and after me. Whatever their motivation, it's getting fucking annoying.*

Jakob Fugger had lived far too long to be scared, but let's start at the beginning.

# CHAPTER 2

# LIFE 1.0 -
# CHILDHOOD AUSTRIA 1459

**B**orn in 1459, Jakob Fugger grew up on a farm outside the city walls of Augsburg in what became Germany but was then Austria.

Like most of the farmers in southern Austria, the Fugger family grew flax, a low green crop that bloomed in periwinkle flowers. Flax mixed with cotton made the most popular fabric of the day. Flax grew in abundance, given the farm's perfect blend of sun, puddles, soil, and manure.

His childhood was pleasant and simple. The family's single-story farmhouse was designed in the style architects refer to as half-timbered post and beam, with white clay and chalk between the dark beams. With its steep thatched roof, most people today think of it as a Hansel and Gretel house. A cluster of oak trees to the south of the farmhouse provided summer shade and cut the winter wind. Around the house's perimeter pink, red, and yellow flowers grew in the summer.

Thick, worn oak planks covered most of the floor. Gray flagstones covered the floor near the massive fireplace and in the kitchen. With a dozen matching oak chairs, the large farm table sat near the fireplace. After sunset, unlike most of its neighbors, the tidy farmhouse's windows were lit with candles for reading. The large house was usually crowded, as Jakob's parents had eleven children that survived childbirth.

Aside from flax, on the farm they raised goats, cows, pigs, and sheep, and on frigid nights, the livestock would sleep in the house, so everything that animals produced, they produced in the farmhouse. On those wintry nights, the pungent scent took several minutes to get used to, but Jakob still found the smell of farm animals comforting.

Jakob, the youngest of the seven boys, loved the farm. One older brother, a lanky, impish prankster, would sometimes arrange the goats and sheep in a semicircle so they all faced away from their youngest sister, knowing precisely what she would awake to discover. He claimed it was to supplement her character, but she argued she had more than enough character.

One frigid night as Jakob's brother bent over, tying a goat's foot to that of the sheep next to it, to ensure their sister awoke to a winter bouquet of buttocks, she had been feigning sleep, and she stabbed him in the rear with a sharpened stick she'd been hiding in her bed for days. Despite the formidable amount of blood, the farmhouse erupted in laughter, and everyone called him "Two Holes" after that.

Jakob's grandfather had been a peasant farmer, but in an impressive and rare status change, Jakob's father became a successful weaver. The Fugger family had become prosperous enough to have a small house in the city, which Jakob's father used as the base of his weaving business. The family even had their own coat of arms. Blue and gold lilies covered a blue and gold shield with further blue and gold ornamentation. Nobody liked the design, but having a coat of arms conveyed a stamp of royal approval and was useful for business.

Another norm in fifteenth-century Austria was for a firstborn son to be named after his father, but for reasons he never shared, Jakob's father waited until his seventh son came along to name him Jakob.

Two Holes and six of Jakob's other siblings died before they could marry. In a world of antibiotics, hospitals, and technological cures, that sounds unbearably tragic. However, in the fifteenth century, it was the norm. Parents had many children because so many of them died young, and having children was retirement planning. Frequently, parents died young as well.

Built like a shopkeeper, Jakob the Elder, as the townspeople referred to Jakob's father, was the strongest man for miles. Nobody exercised then. Born strong, he proved much stronger than the Augsburg blacksmith who had arms like a man's leg.

An old man with many missing teeth who lived on a nearby farm, told young Jakob the story about how his father met his mother, as they sat in a tavern that smelled sweetly of fresh hay. "When your father was a young man, like most weavers, he was constantly thirsty. The dust from weaving gets in your throat, as you well know. Like everyone else in Augsburg, he went to a tavern for beer. We filter the water used to make our beer so it's much cleaner than the well water, and we drink in abundance, for our health, of course.

"One day, Johan the blacksmith was showing off in this very tavern for a pretty young girl with chestnut, flowing hair and a big smile. Her father ran the Augsburg Mint. Johan was trying to impress her with feats of strength. He lifted tables and kegs to show off how strong he was, but it was not having a swoon-inducing effect on her. Rather than change his approach, he left the tavern and came back with a pig, lifting it into his arms and carrying it to the entryway. The pig was huge, and Johan's face and neck were red with effort. His veins stood out, and his eyes grew bloodshot. With the pig in his arms, he blocked the doorway as he caught his breath, waiting for her to notice.

"That was when your father walked up, said 'Excuse me,' and lifted them both out of the way. He then calmly walked in to order a beer." The old man laughed until he coughed and coughed until he nearly fainted. The man continued, "The funny thing is, your dad was the one to marry that girl."

Young Jakob laughed with him when he said, "You were born because of that pig."

Nobody, including Jakob Fugger himself, knows why he didn't die in the sixteenth century, or why he hasn't died since. In the last twenty years alone, he's run every DNA test possible, testing his cells and microbiome. He's been PET scanned, x-rayed, and had his bone marrow tested. He's had brain MRIs, sonograms, EKGs, EEGs, and comprehensive blood panels. Every indication is that he is medically normal with a biological age of 37. He never smoked. His diet is occasionally indulgent. His wine consumption is frequently indulgent. And although he exercises, it is neither consistent nor particularly vigorous. There is literally nothing out of the ordinary about Jakob except that he was born over 560 years ago.

# CHAPTER 3

# LIFE 18.0 - NORTHERN VIRGINIA 2021

After changing routes on the Washington Metro five times, each time changing his gait and minimizing the transit cameras' ability to capture his face, Jakob climbed the stairs to emerge in L'Enfant Plaza in Washington, DC. He quickly stepped into a souvenir shop and purchased an "I heart DC" hoodie, a hat, and several pairs of cheap sunglasses. He put on the hoodie and sunglasses before flagging down a cab and giving the driver an address near his house in northern Virginia.

Serenaded by the cyclical call and response of cicadas, he walked the last five blocks through the tree-lined streets to his house rather than having the cab drop him off. By the time he arrived, a sheen of perspiration from the humidity coated his skin. In a neighborhood of mansions, Jakob's small house faced west over a bend in the Potomac River. Unlike the massive houses up the road, his house had no gate or expansive manicured lawn visible from the road. Bordered on both sides with wooded lots, his was a well-kept modest yard. Despite the efforts of developers to find out who owned the lots, none had discovered that the wooded plots indirectly belonged to Jakob.

At the house, he used the retinal scanner to get inside and stood in front of the sliding glass doors that overlooked the river as he called Hartmann. "Hi, it's me. I need help to figure out who is after me."

Hartmann was the head of Jakob's security team in the US. Several years earlier, Jakob had purchased the company Hartmann worked for and found Hartmann so impressive, he made Hartmann the vice president in charge of his personal security. Hartmann had previously worked with the Swiss Guard at the Vatican and was highly skilled. Jakob spoke to him on a secure voice-over-IP line Hartmann had secured.

Hartmann knew Jakob's voice and replied, "Hello, sir, you had trouble?" His slight Swiss accent, and his concern, were clear on the line.

Pacing over the textured orange carpet, Jakob sighed, "Yes, I almost got picked up at the Reagan National Airport and barely escaped. It turns out I wasn't being paranoid when I thought I was being tailed in the Gare du Nord in Paris a month ago. I'm also pretty certain that the month before that, the men dressed like mercenaries who were intently searching for someone at the Ferrovia train station in Venice were looking for me."

Dropping into a brown upholstered chair, Jakob continued, "They're clearly well-resourced and have tie-ins to intelligence agencies and the police. It could be the CIA, MI-6, or Israel's Mossad, or it could just be someone who's rich enough to buy this access and wants to capture me to get richer."

He could not mention the possibility that he was being chased because he hadn't died in five and a half centuries. He trusted Hartmann with his security, but he trusted nobody with that information.

Jakob found it ironic that several hundred years ago, he had arranged and paid for 150 Swiss Guards to go to the Vatican and provide Pope Julius II with protection. Though neutral today, in the fifteenth century, the Swiss were the most feared warriors in Europe. The guards were ferocious, well-trained, and professional. Jakob envisioned them providing Julius II with an invisible protective wall.

However, Pope Julius II, affiliated with the Medici banking family of Tuscany that saw Jakob's banks as competitors, had something very different in mind. The pope had outfits designed for the Swiss Guards that were as visible as possible with bright orange, red and purple stripes, with baggy arms and legs. Their helmets were black metal and sported a mohawk of red feathers.

Instead of a polite, "Thank you, Jakob, for this gift," Pope Julius II conveyed a very clear, "Screw you, Jakob," by using the Medici colors in their outfits. It may have been the banking rivalry, but Jakob suspected that Pope Julius II didn't enjoy having to pay back the money he'd borrowed from Jakob. Jakob took no small delight when his Austrian banks grew to six times the size of the Medici banks at their peak.

Fashion aside, the Swiss Guards' security skills and attention to detail impressed Jakob considerably.

Hartmann quietly cleared his throat and brought Jakob back to the task at hand. Jakob said, "I'd like your team to check to see if there's an Interpol Red Notice out on me. Also, dig to see what you can find out about who is after me. I authorize expenditures up to three hundred thousand dollars without my further authorization. Without raising too many red flags, reach out to our friends in the intelligence community, and check the dark web. Finally, at sunset, I'd like to meet at the park where we've met before, and please bring some signal scanners."

Four hours later, as the sun painted the sky in pink and gray swaths, Hartmann's team met Jakob at the large softball park. They were wearing exercise outfits and carrying sports duffel bags and water bottles.

"Hello, sir," said Hartmann quietly, as his team started stretching. "How can we help?" The smell of fresh-cut grass and the acidic tang of fertilizer filled the evening air. The park held dozens of people, but they were all in their own virtual bubbles created by their headphones or smartphones.

Jakob followed Hartmann's lead, and spoke softly, "I'd like you to scan me for any sort of monitoring devices that were placed on me or that I may have ingested. I also need suggestions for defeating facial recognition when I travel."

He stretched against a bench as two of the security team subtly waved sets of electronic wands over him, changing the scan frequency with each pass. "You're clean," one announced.

"Thanks, I'd expected that, but wanted to be sure."

Hartmann began, "There are five ways to defeat facial recognition, six if you include cosmetic surgery, but the five quick ways are: One, use a very dark bronzer because the calibration of the systems is based on Caucasians, and even a deep tan bumps up the error rate. Two, use an electronic jammer that will block electronics in a sphere about fifty feet in radius around you. Three, use a cream containing nearly translucent sparkles that reflect light and confuse the cameras, but people don't notice. Four, wear different-colored shapes and lines on your face, which will confuse cameras but draw massive attention to you because you will look like an abstract painting. And five, wear a hat with small LED projectors that shine lights on your face and change the shadows to throw off the cameras."

"Did you say sparkles?" Jakob asked, eyebrow cocked.

"Yes, sir," responded Hartmann. "Facial recognition analysts discovered that young Asian girls who use sparkles in their makeup cause cascading errors in facial recognition software," he continued.

"And with the sparkles, would I have to wear a 'My Little Pony' backpack?"

"Entirely up to you," Hartmann said with a straight face. "Thorough testing has found that Peachy Pie backpacks seem to provide the most protection, although Hello Kitty is still a favorite with tweens."

The two associates laughed so loudly and suddenly that Jakob couldn't match Hartmann's straight face.

"Please get me the supplies I'd need for the jammer, sparkles, and high-tech hat?" Jakob asked when he stopped laughing. He shook his head as he thought about the stereotype that the Swiss have no sense of humor.

"Certainly," Hartmann said, "though I would suggest using the jammer only in dire situations because, while it blocks facial recognition, if the camera is in range, it is the electronic equivalent of setting off a fire alarm. You will get attention."

Jakob shook his hand and replied, "I'll be careful. Thanks. Let me know what you can uncover."

"Very well. Have a nice day, sir."

"You too, Hartmann."

Jakob gave a quick smile to Hartmann's men, doing pushups on the grass, and got the slightest acknowledgment from each.

As he left the park, he looked for overwatch points around the park and gave a slight nod to the rooftops of nearby buildings. From two of the buildings, he got brief flashes of light in response. Jakob smiled to himself and spoke aloud to a squirrel sitting on the park bench as he passed, "I am getting better at this."

# CHAPTER 4

# LIFE 1.0 - THE EMPEROR'S CLOTHES
# AUSTRIA 1468

Germany and Austria in the fifteenth century weren't countries like they are today. They were a collection of small principalities, somewhat like counties in an American state today. The Holy Roman Emperor ruled these German and Austrian counties.

Augsburg was then a free imperial city in Bavaria. Although it sounds like obscure trivia, Augsburg's status proved key to Jakob's success. It meant no bishop, baron, or lord could tax its citizens enough to keep them in poverty.

Further, nobody could commit the town's boys and men to an army. Only the Holy Roman Emperor could do that, but he didn't. Freed from arbitrary taxes and the draft, Augsburg had become a breeding ground for capitalism and a significant crossroads in Germania.

People across Europe lived their whole lives and never saw the emperor, whereas, by the age of 20, Jakob had met the emperor several times. The Holy Roman Emperor was not the pope. He was the regent of Germany and Austria. But he couldn't afford to keep a standing army and didn't have the power of the kings of England, Spain, or France.

The import and export of cloth made Augsburg more international than other towns just a short distance away. Its economy was based on weaving fabric from imported cotton and flax that grew nearby. Unlike almost every other town in Europe, the Black Death that killed 25 million people in Europe a century before had skipped Augsburg. This godsend helped the Augsburg economy even a century later. Whereas most other towns had to start from utter devastation, Augsburg had a running start.

Today, it is a small city of no particular importance. It sits closer to Munich on the road between Munich and Stuttgart. Ironically, it is most famous for an affordable housing complex for workers that Jakob built five centuries before, called the Fuggerai.

The Fuggerai's high-quality houses are still in use today, and their rent has never increased, making living there almost free. When Jakob built them, the homes in the Fuggerai were not free, but were far less expensive than anything nearby. He built them to help the workers, and because he needed workers.

In the fifteenth century, it was a regional center of commerce frequented by the most influential people of the day, but Augsburg's importance faded with time.

In contrast to the farm, Jakob's father's weaving shop in Augsburg was impeccable. Dirt was bad for the cloth business, and business was all-important. Jakob's father ran the business well because of his careful and diligent work, but Jakob's mother drove much of the growth of his business.

Jakob the Elder drove himself to improve his lot in life and worked very hard, whereas his wife was simply brilliant. She had a head for business and figures. The Elder aspired to become one of the top merchants in Augsburg, which published its tax rolls each year, making it clear who was wealthy and who was not. To most townspeople, topping the list was a major accomplishment.

But Jakob's mother had much grander ambitions for the family. She wanted the family to work with kings, bishops, princes, and popes and have business interests throughout Europe. Her goals seemed inconceivable to her husband, but young Jakob thought her goals seemed attainable given enough time, and her goals became his.

She was wily. She would ask the Elder questions to plant ideas.

"Emperor Frederick II and his son Maximilian are coming to Augsburg soon, are they not?" she asked one night as she placed meat pies over a roaring fire in the massive fireplace. She acted as though she didn't already know the answer.

Not realizing it was a setup, he continued to drink his beer before he replied, "Yes, in a few weeks. Why do you ask?"

"I heard Maximilian is going to ask for the princess's hand in marriage from her father, the King of Burgundy." She threw an unnecessary log on the fire.

Paying more attention to his beer than the conversation, he responded, "Yes, that should be quite an event."

"So true," she replied. "The King of Burgundy is very wealthy, and I am sure he and his court will wear amazing clothing. I wonder if Frederick and Maximilian have clothing that would even compare."

Frederick II, the Holy Roman Emperor, perpetually overspent his treasury. Part of the reason for his plan to engage his son to the

17

Princess of Burgundy was accessing the overflowing Burgundian treasury.

"I do not know," Jakob's father said, paying closer attention only because the conversation had turned to clothes.

"If someone wanted to win favor from the current emperor and his son, the future emperor… Might that person give them some amazing clothing, so they look splendid in Burgundy?" She went back to checking her dinner as if the conversation had finished. The delicious smell of meat pies filled the farmhouse as she took them off the flames. Though meat was rare in European meals except on special occasions, the Fuggers were wealthy enough to have it with dinner twice a week. Ironically, for those living near a city, it was a luxury to eat at home. The cost of wood and coal made it less expensive for many to eat at communal tables with food from a large kitchen.

"You know, my love," the Elder announced minutes later as young Jakob sat down to eat with the family, "I have an idea. I think I shall make two of the finest suits I have ever made and give them to the Holy Roman Emperor and his son."

As innocent as an angel, she said, "Oh? Would that not be an expensive gift?" Young Jakob looked at her, wondering why she hadn't pointed out that his father had just parroted back her own idea. But she gave him a quick glance and a slight smile. Then he understood her plan.

"It will be expensive, but we can afford it," he assured her, "and think of the benefits of having the emperor in our debt!"

Her idea was right beyond all measure. Maximilian fell in love with the Princess of Burgundy and replaced his father as the Holy

Roman Emperor. Those two suits gave the Fugger family its first solid connection with the Hapsburgs of Austria, as Maximilian was a Hapsburg. It formed the basis of the family's wealth creation for decades.

CHAPTER 5


# LIFE 18.0 -
# TIME TO GO VIRGINIA 2021


"It is time for me to leave. The video surveillance we set up around my neighborhood is picking up slow-moving SUVs with heavily tinted windows near my street," Jakob said to Hartmann, as he got up from one of his brown armchairs.

"And before you tell me, yes, I know the areas around Washington DC are awash with tinted SUVs, so I wasn't alarmed at first. But they have been running what looks like a search pattern for two days. I assume they are searching for unencrypted data leakage or hoping I would blithely cross the street in front of them."

The fiber feed directly into Jakob's white cottage with black shutters on the Potomac made electronic signal leakage a non-concern. All internet traffic was first encrypted, then routed through multilayer virtual private networks, making attempts at interception extremely difficult and the detection of his exact location impossible. Despite his electronic precautions, someone had found his neighborhood.

*They must have spent days going over the footage from the Metro, then tracked down the taxi.*

Jakob's office inside the house was a Faraday cage with an array of batteries he used when working, so he was off the grid. The floors, walls, and ceiling were lined with copper mesh to stop even a high-powered electromagnetic pulse or EMP from wiping out his computers. The mesh further ensured there were no electronic signals seeping out. When he closed the office door from the inside, the battery array in the room provided the power. He was completely disconnected from the outside world, except for the single strand of fiber.

Hartmann's team designed the setup. He said, "I am not concerned that someone will find you by electronically sniffing your neighborhood. I am, however, concerned that if they are going to that level of trouble and expense, they are doing much more than just driving around."

Jakob replied, "That concerns me too. Please call our pilots and tell them to prepare for Operation Trading Places in a few hours? Finally, I wonder if you could bring the items we discussed and meet me at the house with two of your men in an hour?"

"See you then," said Hartmann, disconnecting the call.

Jakob had been living in his current identity, using his original sixteenth-century name, for almost twenty-eight years. Soon, it would be time to build another identity. Every thirty to thirty-five years, Jakob had to assume a new identity, or else his not aging became too difficult to disguise.

In the early 1990s, he began to refer to his past lives as Life 1.0, Life 2.0, and so on. He had been quite proud of his naming convention, as it seemed clever at the time because software updates were coming out as version 2.0, and 3.0. Despite now living Life

18.0, and the cleverness having been very short-lived, he still mentally used the naming convention when thinking about his past identities.

That evening, three cars pulled up and parked in different spots on Jakob's street. The sky carried the threat of a thunderstorm, which made the air feel almost liquid. Hartmann and his associates arrived at Jakob's door; he entered a code that required his biometrics before opening, and the three men entered. They carried the items Jakob had requested. Hartmann, true to form, put the sparkling skin cream in a bright orange Peachy Pie My Little Pony backpack, which he proffered to Jakob with a completely straight face.

Jakob just lowered his head in resignation when he saw it. Hartmann had once again outdone him in the stupid-joke department.

"Any updates on your research?" Jakob asked the group, trying not to smile.

One of Hartmann's lieutenants replied, "Yes sir, our current hypothesis is that this is not coming from a western government. We don't think it is China, nor does it appear to be the Middle East. We can't, however, rule out countries from the former Soviet Union."

"Russia?"

"We are unsure. Private bulletin boards on the dark web list jobs for mercenaries in English and the syntax is not that of a native English-speaker. The errors are one step up from those Google Translate would generate."

As they discussed tactics, they watched the video cameras. A second Suburban joined the sole black Suburban that had been stalking the neighborhood. One car stalked Jakob's street almost constantly, moving from house to house, then slowly moving past. A Suburban slowed in front of Jakob's driveway and, seemingly reluctantly, slowly pulled away.

Jakob and Hartmann's men used that as their signal to act. As the black Suburban pulled away, the four men walked out of Jakob's house together. Each wore dark shoes, dark pants, a baggy dark blue windbreaker, and gray baseball caps. Each also carried a dark duffel bag. The three others wore fifteen-dollar hats, but with the LED electronics embedded in Jakob's, he figured his cost more like $150,000. When he saw his reflection in one of the agent's sunglasses, Jakob didn't recognize himself. His nose looked smaller, his mouth larger, and he appeared to have a stronger chin courtesy of the lights in the hat.

He walked to his assigned car and in his peripheral vision saw the Suburban driver trying to pivot the massive SUV on the small street. It was drizzling, which muted the sound of the river nearby and made details hard to see. Jakob opened the door of his prearranged car and started it up. Hartmann climbed into an Uber that had been waiting for him, while the two others walked to the cars they drove to get to Hartmann's house. Anyone surveying the area saw four men dressed identically, simultaneously leaving and driving similar dark sedans in different directions. The mercenaries had no idea who to follow.

The black Suburban spun its wheels once it turned around and raced towards the four cars. Jakob and the three decoys passed a second black Suburban speeding to assist the first as they approached the on-ramp to the GW parkway. Unfortunately for the second SUV, it headed in the wrong direction. Two of the decoy cars went west towards the Beltway, Jakob headed east towards DC, and the third decoy car continued south towards downtown McLean, Virginia. Both black SUVs arrived at the parkway on-ramps at the same time. Jakob watched in his car's rearview mirror as a muscular man in black got out and threw his hands up in the air in frustration.

*Is there some unwritten rule that bad guys must dress in black and have enormous arms?*

Jakob drove from northern Virginia into Washington, DC, stopping briefly in the tunnels that ran under the Senate, where he switched his car for a motorcycle. The Suzuki rested on the small berm of the road with one of Hartmann's men pretending to struggle with it.

To a chorus of beeping horns and screeching brakes, Jakob quickly put on the helmet, started the motorcycle, and turned around in the underground structure. Hartmann's man, who had been pretending to fix the motorcycle, jumped into the car Jakob had been driving and sped away. Jakob came back out the way he entered, unidentifiable in a black motorcycle helmet. Fortunately, the rain had stopped, otherwise, he would have been soaked.

From DC, he drove into Maryland, then back to Virginia, ending up at Signature Aviation, the private airport next to Reagan National Airport. The guard at the gate expected him, so he pulled the bike onto the tarmac, and the private turboprop plane took off five minutes later, flying west. All private flight was expensive, but Jakob's Germanic thrift still influenced his choices. Although he could afford jets, he liked turboprops; he found when flying less than five hours, the door-to-door time saved using jets versus turboprops wasn't worth the extra millions.

Over Ohio, they flew near Jakob's similar-looking turboprop plane flying south 1,000 feet below them. After Jakob's pilot sent a brief message to the pilot of the second plane, they traded transponder codes, and the second plane turned to the west while Jakob's plane turned to the south. As far as air traffic control knew, both planes continued their originally filed flight plans after their radar blips got close to one another. Sitting in the supremely comfortable seat, finishing the last of his shrimp cocktail, Jakob inhaled the light citrus smell of the air conditioning in the plane and continued to work on his laptop as he flew towards Florida.

After an hour of work in the quiet interior of the plane, Jakob reclined his seat completely and looked out at a distant cloud formation.

*It is getting expensive to stay free.*

# CHAPTER 6

# LIFE 1.0 -
# EVERYONE SINS AUSTRIA 1469

Although his father ran a merchant house, Jakob learned about business from his mother. She knew how to plan, calculate, save, budget, bribe, flatter, and be discreet. Jakob the Elder was a good man, but his strengths were his muscles and his work ethic. Jakob's mother's strength was her mind as she understood things without being taught. She could read and write German, Latin, French, Holland Dutch, Spanish, and English. And she could understand even more languages.

Few women read in the fifteenth century, and fewer were skilled at mathematics. Yet, Barbara Fugger could figure, extrapolate, and she could teach. Her prized possession was an algebra book, a Latin translation of the Arabian *Al-Jabr* that Jakob's father gave her on their wedding night. She loved him all the more for it.

At age 10, Jakob left the farmhouse and moved inside the walls of Augsburg. His father had moved into a larger home, and as the home represented his business, it stayed immaculate. Augsburg in the 1460s was a beautiful town. A walled city with tall towers and multistoried buildings, the winding streets were picturesque.

Though it had no castle, it looked like the town now pictured in children's storybooks featuring princesses in need of a rescue. A large dose of German obsessive-compulsive disorder kept the city tidy and pretty, with colorful flowers streaming out of window boxes in warm weather. It also kept the city smelling good, particularly compared to other cities that smelled like outhouses.

Augsburg was also a very Catholic town. Everyone ruled by the Holy Roman Emperor was devoutly Catholic. The townspeople were certain that God's son, Jesus, died for their sins. They knew that if they lived a good life with few sins, they would go to purgatory, which is essentially heaven's waiting area, where they would suffer to be cleansed of their sins before they ascended to heaven. They didn't doubt that if they died having committed too many sins, they would spend eternity burning in hellfire while Satan devised new tortures for their souls. Further, they were certain that the pope was the direct successor of the Apostle Peter, appointed by Jesus, and imbued with immense powers, including the ability to forgive any sin. These religious truths were as real to them as their knowledge that the sun rose and set.

The pope, when running out of funds, would occasionally allow sinners to have their sins forgiven by purchasing an indulgence, a script authorized by him, to forgive sins in his name. The pope was currently selling indulgences in Germany, and this gave Jakob's mother, Barbara, an idea.

"Everyone sins. Am I right?" she asked one night after dinner as the family sat around the massive cooking fireplace in the Augsburg house. Jakob's father, now more used to her tactics, became alert immediately as he agreed.

"And sinners suffer in purgatory for their sins, which is torturous, correct?"

Confused and wary, he again agreed.

"One way to reduce time suffering in purgatory is through thousands of hours of prayer," she asserted, "unless the Church is selling indulgences. Because if you buy an indulgence, you avoid purgatory. Correct?"

He nodded, still with no idea where her questions would lead.

"By coincidence, the Church is selling indulgences throughout Germania, but they need the money to get back to the Vatican in Rome. Yes?" Jakob's father nodded cautiously.

"But aren't the priests afraid of carrying money to Rome?" his mother asked as his father smiled.

"Why yes, they are. Robbers would beset them," he replied.

Highway robbery in the sixteenth century didn't mean you were overcharged. It was literal. There were few good roads, and those roads were populated with gangs of robbers that would relieve travelers of their possessions. On the multi-day trip from Austria to Rome, a traveler would encounter robbers.

"A merchant that already had caravans of cloth going to Rome and who had already bribed the robbers for passage might transport the money to Rome for a fee, wouldn't that merchant?"

Jakob the Elder now stood, excited. "That merchant might well be able to do it!"

"If that merchant was married to a beautiful maiden with a brother in Rome, said brother could arrange for the contract, yes?"

Jakob's father gathered her up into his arms and kissed her. "That merchant is married to a beautiful maiden, and she is brilliant!"

29

Children weren't the only ones that died regularly, and Jakob the Elder died that year, just before Jakob turned 11. It would be a decade before young Jakob would get his own nickname, Jakob the Rich.

Barbara Fugger was also industrious. She took over running the family's profitable weaving and gold-transporting business with Jakob and his older brothers. She taught all of them about business as she made decisions and improved the business. Jakob was her favorite student, as learning was an insatiable hunger for him. The more he learned, the more he wanted to know.

He learned how to think and analyze from her. When they lived on the farm, she showed him that most people planted and worked just enough to get by if everything went well. Farm work never ended, so Jakob understood this. Nobody was looking for additional work. But, when things went poorly, through a poor harvest, injury, or death, many families barely made it to the next planting, and some didn't.

Her lessons were informal and Socratic. As she and Jakob walked the fields of flax, pointing to the west, she said, "Our neighbor Schmidt has three young children, and he farms to feed them."

Then, pointing north, she continued, "Herr Eichenlaub has six children. Does Eichenlaub work twice as many hours as Schmidt?"

Jakob thought about that for a long time before he responded, "They both work from sunrise to after sunset, but if Schmidt worked more like Eichenlaub, he would have more than he needs, and he could save the extra food.

"But, Mother," he then argued, thinking he'd discovered a rare flaw in her logic, "if you do not eat the extra food in time, it will rot."

"That is true," she said, "if you store the surplus as food. But you can sell the food and store it as these." She pulled out two gold florins, the common currency.

Storing food as money was an eye-opening concept for Jakob. Florins could convert to food, and food could convert to florins. "You could even use the florins to buy things other than food," he blurted, "like a neighbor's land, and more flax and cotton, and then store those gains as florins."

She smiled, "Smart! You are thinking strategically." Jakob glowed with pride. The highest compliment his mother ever gave was calling someone smart.

"Can florins," she asked, "grow other florins?" She said no more, and Jakob, not quite 11 years old, stood pondering her question.

The next day, when she returned from the market, Jakob waited for her. "Florins can grow other florins!"

She lifted an eyebrow, so he continued, "You can lend florins to someone else. They will repay with interest, so you end up with more florins than you started with. Banks grow florins!" Banks in the fifteenth century differed greatly from those today. In many towns, a bank was little more than a moneylender who would position himself behind a large board, called a bank, and negotiate over it.

She smiled and said, "Precisely!"

Making money from money was a dangerous subject in the sixteenth century. The Church had decreed it the sin of usury to lend money for interest. But almost everyone borrowed money, ironically including bishops, cardinals, and the pope. Making a loan with interest carried danger, as it only took one priest to claim usury, and the lender would be in trouble with both the government and the Church.

# CHAPTER 7

# LIFE 18.0 - FLORIDA 2021

As he flew south on his way to Florida, Jakob's attempts to refocus on accounting proved futile as thoughts about his current predicament kept interrupting. Finally, he decided just to think it through.

*Why is someone trying to capture me? I have broken no laws, so there is no legitimate law enforcement reason. I'm wealthy, so I can't rule out a kidnapping, but the former Soviet connection makes me think it may be an attempt to extort me.*

*The issue that I can't discuss with anyone is my age. It isn't impossible that someone has figured out that I haven't aged in five centuries, and they want the secret that keeps me alive. But chances of someone knowing that are so small, it can't be the reason.*

Jakob had never been seriously sick and healed quickly. He'd never been in battle, had a riding accident, car accident, drowned, been shot or stabbed, or in some other way irreparably damaged his body. However, he had been stoned, which nearly proved deadly, but he survived, unmaimed but in excruciating pain. Jakob didn't know if he would die from severe bodily trauma, and though somewhat curious about it, he was not curious enough to risk dying. Dying didn't scare him as much as being seriously harmed and living hundreds of years in constant pain.

*I have a lot yet to do, and I'm not ready to die.*

Jakob held himself responsible for starting a war that killed millions, and he was determined to use his time and wealth to make up for that overarching sin. He spent centuries trying to help people, and though he diligently tried, it proved difficult. Despite all his efforts, people overcame almost any good he tried to do.

Jakob's introspection led to fitful sleep on the plane, and he woke up from a vivid dream of the girl he met 540 years ago, but never even spoke to. In his dream, they were together, walking and holding hands as she laughed. In the dream, he went to kiss her, his hand behind her neck pulling her mouth to his; then he woke up. It was a recurring dream, and he had yet to kiss her in it, though he could still feel the warmth of her neck on his fingers.

*I feel trapped in a Bollywood movie. Almost, but never quite kissing the girl.*

He tried to hold on to the warm feel of her neck in his hand, but like always, it faded.

Once awake, he worked for the rest of the flight. The plane came in for a landing at the small airport as the sun descended to the horizon. He closed the laptop and watched the light fade through the small window. As the plane's stairs opened after landing, it felt as if Florida was competing with Virginia for the highest humidity. Damp air washed into the plane, carrying with it the smell of lush plants and a hint of the ocean salt. Jakob ducked out the exit, thanked the pilots, and asked them to set up for another transponder swap.

In the minute it took Jakob to cross to the car waiting on the tarmac, he'd already started sweating. The driver, standing by an unremarkable light blue sedan waiting on the tarmac, yelled over the sound of a plane taking off, "Hello, sir. Welcome to Florida in the summer."

They drove for about forty minutes, getting on and off highways and circling back repeatedly to reach Jakob's Florida house. It would only have taken seven minutes if he hadn't been trying to lose a tail. In the car, Jakob reviewed the rest of the financials.

Having started in business before accounting was in regular use, modern accounting software still seemed almost magical to him. He could see the consolidated operations of his different businesses and investments in one spot on a laptop, something it had taken his teams of accountants weeks to produce for him a long time ago.

He thought back to when he'd returned to Augsburg from Venice in Life 1.0 as a teenager. He'd gone to Venice to learn how they handled business. Back in Augsburg, and back in business full time, he explained to his bookkeepers that he wanted to use double-entry accounting, something they had never heard of. He further wanted to merge the reporting across the family's different businesses in Germania, France, Hungary, and the Italian city-states.

Even the Venetians had never done that. His bookkeepers looked at him as if he were asking them to levitate while turning lead into gold. However, after several days of Jakob doing the accounting himself and showing them what he meant, one by one they caught on. While they would never levitate, Jakob grew confident they could help him turn his little treasury of gold into a lot more gold.

Jakob smiled at the memory as the car pulled into the garage of his Florida home. He thanked the driver before he entered the code and stood for the retinal scanner. Only when the door from the garage to the house opened did the car pull away. The driver, one of Hartmann's men, took security seriously.

The door to his office in his Florida home was hidden, and the security was hard to spot. Once inside, it was like his other ones, with the copper mesh, banks of batteries and a fiber feed. He entered and closed the door, activating the battery array. Only then did he connect his laptop into the secure internet and let the work he'd completed on the plane percolate out to the internet. Despite the temptation of Wi-Fi everywhere, he'd spent too much time around hackers in the last twenty years to trust it. So, when he used a laptop in public or on a plane, he used it in airplane mode.

Jakob knew his success depended on information. He built his first information network in the late fifteenth century. At the time, it involved men, women, horses, ships, bribes, threats, pigeons, handwritten codes, and hundreds of spies. It took him a decade to establish and an exorbitant amount of money to keep working, but it worked well.

From his small back office in the Augsburg building owned by his brothers, Jakob knew the outcome of battles before kings did. The prices of silk, pepper, silver, and gold in six different countries were updated daily. Loans made by the Medicis and other banking competitors were tracked. Jakob knew the currencies and their relative values, as well as the most recent location of hundreds of ships with their likely cargo and their intended destinations. He knew who slept with whom in the emperor's court, the Spanish king's court, the courts of Burgundy, Venice, Paris, and in the Church. He had insight into the political maneuvering in all of them.

Because of his web of informants, Jakob could know of events that happened in another country mere days after they had happened. This information gave him an edge that helped him become the richest man in Europe at the time. Some went so far as to claim he was the richest man in the world.

CHAPTER 8

# LIFE 1.0 - INVESTING AUGSBURG 1470

Outwardly, Jakob's mother was devout, but she questioned Church doctrine on almost everything except their stance on being kind to others, killing, adultery, lying, and stealing. Jakob agreed with her.

Admittedly, it's odd to say that a young child agreed with his mother about something as abstract as religious philosophy. The default assumption is that the parent's influence defines the child's beliefs. However, Jakob was no ordinary child. By the time he was 9, Jakob and his mother discussed, as equals, religion and Church doctrine almost as much as they discussed finance. Neither of them believed lending money for interest was a sin. They believed it was good.

However, she influenced Jakob's view of commerce. She would take Jakob into the market in Augsburg, where they watched the haggling, deliveries, merchants, and Jakob's favorite, the moneylenders. The market thrived as barely controlled chaos. Filled with animals, produce, and people, none of whom washed regularly, the market was pungent, dirty, loud, and exciting.

As they observed the transactions, Barbara would point out the strategies, the bluffs, and the lies involved. She noted the different prices paid by trusted men compared to those who weren't. Frequently, she would ask Jakob about the risks of a specific transaction they'd observed and expect a detailed, nuanced answer.

She loved the negotiation, but Jakob loved learning how the men used the money they were borrowing. He wanted to learn how they would earn enough to pay it back and still be better off. For centuries, even kings gained their wealth through taking assets from someone else by force. Few considered that there were alternatives. Investing and working harder and smarter weren't as appealing as seizing things that belonged to others. Might equaled right.

Credit changed that.

Some men who came to the moneylenders in the Augsburg market were idiots. They could never repay, but they had collateral. A few of the lenders specialized in this and would lend florins, expecting they would own the collateral.

Other bankers lent for the interest. They were more conservative, lending only to men who barely needed the money, had collateral, and had someone to vouch for them. Both strategies were viable. Jakob and his mother would stand still and quietly listen. A woman and a boy posed no threat, and most entirely forgot they were even there. Then, after a transaction, she would quiz Jakob about it.

"Herr Lorenz just made a thousand florins on that deal. What are his risks now?" Jakob's mother asked.

She knew the obvious ones, so he had to dig deeper. "Herr Lorenz has to travel to Venice to buy more silk and bring it back here to sell it," Jakob responded. "If he travels with that much money and he gets robbed, they will take it all unless he can arrange bribes before he goes."

"And?" She opened her hands as if wanting more.

The surrounding cacophony seemed to quiet as Jakob thought it through. "If he gets to Venice and buys the silk, he still has to carry it back. He runs the same risks of robbery and tolls. If he is not careful and lucky, he could lose everything," Jakob responded proudly.

But it didn't end there. "So, what should he do?"

Jakob ran different scenarios through his mind. As his mother rose to leave, he answered her.

"Herr Lorenz should get a letter of exchange from an Augsburg bank that he can redeem in Venice—that eliminates the threat of robbery. Once he is in Venice, rather than spend it all on silk, he should keep cash to bribe the robbers for the trip back, or to buy his way into a caravan that already has."

Other boys played on the periphery of the market, running, using sticks as swords, and wrestling one another, but none had as much fun as Jakob.

"My, you are smart," she said. As they talked more on the way back to the house, his mother said that if she were a moneylender, she would want the interest and part of the upside of the business. That seemed smart to Jakob.

His mother mentioned compounding in their discussions, and until Jakob turned 11, he didn't know what she meant. One day it just clicked. In his excitement, he told his older brother Two Holes, "If you invest, and you get back more than you invested through interest or profit, and then you invest that gain, the gains will grow bigger each year. That's compounding. If you use compounding and get wealthy enough, you can achieve enough influence to work with popes, kings, and emperors like Mother says. I will use compounding to reach our mother's goals!"

Two Holes said, "Jakob, I don't know what you're talking about, but you will be richer than kings." He wasn't the smartest of the Fugger children, but he was the nicest. Unfortunately, he died the next year.

# CHAPTER 9

# LIFE 18.0 -
# SEARCHING THE NET FLORIDA 2021

The internet can provide much of the information that Jakob had created an army of informants to provide him with, but the internet can do it instantaneously. Unfortunately, the only advantage conveyed by publicly available information came from competition with lazy people. Jakob, therefore, got extra intelligence by maintaining a paid network of informants who keep him aware of items of interest as they happen. It was similar to the one he had in the 1500s. But rather than via ships, horses, and pigeons, this information arrived via email.

Booting up his computers, Jakob checked in to see if Hartmann had any news, and he did. He relaxed into his gaming chair, which proved to be much more comfortable than the high-end leather office chairs he'd had before. After decrypting, Hartmann's email was brief and direct.

Someone is hiring high-end security in large numbers ranging from IT specialists to mercenaries. If hired, they are to find a target(s). The ID of the target(s) is unknown. The pay rate is high, and the resources offered to the mercenaries are extraordinary. There are several teams in major cities across the globe. No additional information is yet available. It's unclear if they are hit-teams or abduction-teams.

*I'm not concerned about hit teams. If the mercenaries had wanted to kill me, they could have already. I am concerned about abduction teams. Extorting a businessperson for $5 million would not justify an effort like this. It probably costs them $5 million per week to keep it going. Only extorting one or several extremely rich people for much of their wealth would justify it.*

*Hartmann doesn't know who is hiring, but it's not the IRS or a Euro taxing authority. They don't hire mercenaries, and I don't owe any taxes. I can rule out the FBI or NSA, who subcontract nothing important, much less hire mercenaries. I can't rule out the CIA, though they don't need money, so why they would care about me is bewildering. I have been careful not to get involved in anything linked to terror or drugs, and I don't work in the CIA's hotspots.*

*I think it's a private party, or a foreign government wants my money or, less likely, wants to vivisect me to ascertain why I don't die.*

*I'm worried because both my true wealth and age should be unknown. I am meticulous in obscuring any connection among my "lives" that could link someone back to my current one.*

In previous centuries, ensuring no thread connected one of his identities to any of his others was simple because there weren't yet computers or networked taxing agencies. With ubiquitous IDs, AI-assisted computer systems, and international banking agreements, it became much more difficult, but not impossible, in the present.

In his offices, Jakob had three screens set up in a semicircle around him which were normally used to monitor news, markets, investments, and research. In his Florida basement office, his screens showed video feeds around his house, searches in public and private databases, and news scans for other wealthy individuals who disappeared.

*I think the reason I'm being chased is that someone is attempting an expanded "oligarch squeeze."*

The oligarch squeeze happened between 2003 and 2005 in Russia. But the conditions for it started years earlier, just after the fall of the Soviet Union in 1991. The economy of Communist USSR, where it was illegal to operate a business for profit, collapsed and a few men emerged from the chaos with immense wealth.

Corrupt governments of the former Soviet countries, clueless about markets, privatized state-owned assets in two ways. The first was through straightforward theft of assets, which were transferred to high-ranking former officers, making those kleptocrats wealthy.

The second may have been inadvertent. To spread the wealth to its citizens, the government issued privatization vouchers that could later be traded for common stock in the former state-owned monopolies. They distributed these to a population clueless about what any of that meant. The people didn't know what common stock meant, what a state-run business was worth, much less what the vouchers might be worth.

The few men who understood this bought those vouchers from the Russian people, frequently for less than a penny on the dollar. There were stories of men buying $50,000 of the former Soviet gas company, Gazprom, vouchers for two bottles of vodka. Instead of the people owning the state enterprise, roughly one hundred men ended up owning the steel plants, mines, energy companies, and factories of the former Soviet countries. With the kleptocrats, they became the oligarchs, and all of them were billionaires.

When Vladimir Putin, the former KGB head, came to power in 2003, he determined the oligarchs needed to share the wealth. Putin didn't want them to share with the people of Russia, but with himself. He drafted bogus laws that effectively made being an oligarch illegal.

He started by squeezing a smaller oligarch named Gusinsky, who fled the country and had his assets seized by Putin. Emboldened, Putin then moved to the richest, and perhaps the only principled oligarch, a man named Mikhail Khodorkovsky. Putin had him arrested and charged with violating the ridiculous laws that Putin had just created.

Khodorkovsky, Russia's richest man with a net worth of about US $15 billion, miscalculated and tried to stand up to Putin. Putin demanded most of his assets to make the trumped-up charges go away. Khodorkovsky felt confident that no court would convict him of such obviously false charges in the new Russia.

New Russia turned out to be Putin's Russia. The court convicted Khodorkovsky, and he forfeited almost all his net worth, most of which ended up in Putin's private accounts. Khodorkovsky spent over eight years in prison, much of which he spent making mittens in a decrepit factory. Putin took over 99% of Khodorkovsky's billions and exiled him after graciously pardoning him months before he completed his sentence. The third oligarch Putin approached with his give-me-half offer, decided half of his wealth was an entirely acceptable amount to pay to stay free and on Putin's good side. So did the other oligarchs Putin squeezed.

With a fraction of the proceeds of his oligarch squeeze, Putin built a summer house on the Black Sea, and a few years later, bought a boat. The summer house cost US $1.2 billion dollars and covers 180,000 square feet. His €500 million boat is 269 feet long and has its own 49-foot-long indoor pool.

*Maybe Putin is expanding his squeeze globally? Already an international reprobate, he could target non-Russians. Or maybe someone else is trying a version of what Putin did?*

In Life 1.0, Jakob became the richest non-royal in Europe, with a net worth equivalent in modern US dollars to that of Elon Musk and Jeff Bezos combined. Several economic historians claim he accounted for over 2% of all of Europe's Gross Domestic Product. In idle moments, Jakob would google himself, and smile as his reported wealth in the 1600s grew each year as historians revised it upward.

He left most of his money and his businesses with his nephews, but a fraction he set aside for Jakob's Life 2.0. In that life, a portion of what he earned, he set aside for Life 3.0, and so on. Because of the compounding returns of over 500 years, Jakob effectively had unlimited funds.

A private man, this required that he design the web of ownership that would be labyrinthian and confusing unless you had the key, which, of course, he did. The complexity of his ownership structures had increased in the last several decades.

In the last thirty years alone, he has established a series of lightly regulated family offices. Each of them had strategically hard to pronounce names. A US government tax investigator is more likely to investigate the Judd Family Office rather than the Sadece Önemsiz Family Office. This is in part because they can't pronounce Turkish words, and in part because most organizations alphabetize their target lists. Jakob has also established a plethora of dynastic trusts, limited liability companies, and their European equivalents, like the Luxembourg *Société à responsabilité limitée simplifiées.*

In all his investments, he is careful to abide by environmental, financial, and employment regulations, and pay all taxes legitimately owed. He doesn't play games with taxes. However, because he doesn't actually die, he is careful to structure his estate to avoid "death taxes." Many of his ventures were in the USA, and in 1916, they started collecting estate taxes. The top rate rose from 10% to 77%. Just before the 1980s, the rates fell to 55% and hovered at or below that since then.

Jakob does not want to draw attention to himself. His worst-case scenario was his name showing up on a Forbes or Bloomberg billionaire list. Particularly in the USA, billionaires are celebrities, and given his aging secret, he preferred the shadows.

*I will need Hartmann to investigate if there is a global oligarch squeeze going on. The connection of the Slavic wording used in the dark web and the possibility that there may be more targets than me makes this my working theory.*

Aside from the family offices, trusts, and LLCs, Jakob has established several charities through which to make positive impacts on the world. Through one of those, he purchased and donated 450,000 acres of forest, spread across the globe, to environmental causes. The forests are lightly managed and occasionally thinned for timber, but otherwise they remain untouched.

However, he grew disappointed by how ineffective many of his charitable activities became. To improve global education, he donated over sixty million dollars to universities worldwide to enable more students to afford excellent education. Rather than reduce the cost of tuition, the universities raised tuition and rolled his donations into their endowments once he had "died." He worked with charities in Africa, Asia, and the Caribbean Islands to help children get better educations. But rather than improve education, they improved the structures and hired more administration.

It seemed as if an industry of people generated feel-good reports for the boards of charitable institutions, which hid failures behind heartwarming tales. Despite the difficulties he encountered, he kept trying, hoping that by helping others, he would partially offset the deaths of millions who died in the Catholic-Protestant wars over the years.

Back in his Florida office, one of his computer screens showed another dark SUV driving on the residential streets, the third one in an hour. Aggravated, he knew the SUV's presence suggested he may have to move again, sooner rather than later.

*Well, crap.*

# CHAPTER 10

# LIFE 1.0 -
# DOUBLE ENTRY ITALY 1473

At 14, Jakob went to Venice to study. Of course, it was his mother's idea. "Learn how the Venetians track the flow of money," she told Jakob. "Numbers and accounts are the language of business, and you must be fluent in them. Nobody understands commerce as well as the Venetians."

Venice overwhelmed him at first. Many times the size of Augsburg, each day the city came alive with trade. With populations of over 160,000 people each, Venice, Naples, and Paris were the three largest cities in Europe in the 1400s. They were more than twice as big as Rome. The canals were beautiful when the tide flowed in, but at low tide, given everything dumped in the canals, the smell could make one's eyes water.

As a native German speaker, Jakob could not stay where he wanted-ed. He slept in the Germanic business offices, far away from the palaces on the Grand Canal. The inelegant business offices proved comfortable and were on a relatively stench-free canal.

The Italian food tasted superb. Jakob grew up eating fried dough and bland German fare slathered with mustard for flavor. In

Venice, flavors and combinations were explosive. Sauces, cheeses, and spices were everywhere, as Venice was the hub of the spice trade. Pepper and even more exotic spices arrived in Venice after traveling by boat and camel from the East. The Venetian chefs took full advantage of easy access to make delicious dishes. At times Jakob still wakes up from a dream about the first meal he ate in Venice.

He had been traveling for eight days with one of his family's cloth and gold caravans. The caravan moved at the pace of a man walking during daylight. Most of the gangs of robbers had accepted bribes for clear passage, but the caravan still risked attack from upstart gangs, and it wasn't uncommon for robbers to take a payoff and rob a caravan anyway. Jakob rode in the front and carried the culverin, a heavy metal tube with one end closed except for a slot to load gunpowder and ignite it. It was a small hand cannon. When they arrived in Venice, he felt exhausted from constant vigilance, and he hadn't eaten in eighteen hours.

Despite his fatigue, after sunset, Jakob and two acquaintances from Augsburg crossed the bridges and smelled an almost erotic scent. Tomatoes, garlic, pepper, and olive oil filled the air with the most amazing smell. They followed the smell to a restaurant with a Napoletano chef and sat outside, drinking wine from Rome. The sounds of Venice were different. The singsong of Italian flowed through the city like the canals. Though he knew several languages, he had never thought of German as a harsh-sounding language until he immersed himself in Italian. The constant lapping of the water against the sides of the canals and the birds competing for the scraps from the fishmongers provided constant background noise.

When their pasta dinners arrived, each bowl was the size of a family serving bowl heaped with pasta in a sauce made with tomatoes, crushed garlic, salt, pepper, and a mix of cheeses. In Augsburg, fish was expensive and saved for religious days, but here scampi, whitefish, and steamed mollusks were woven through the braids of pasta. Finely shredded *Parmigiano Reggiano* cheese coated everything like a slow-melting, delicious warm snow. Fortunately, Venice had adopted the use of forks, as eating pasta with his hands would have proved messy given the red sauce that coated everything. Though his stomach would be distended for a day, he finished the whole bowl. It was unforgettable.

The Venetian art awed him. Jakob enjoyed sitting by the Grand Canal with his coworkers, talking about art and architecture. One night, after too much wine, Jakob said, "The art is nice, but the accounting is equally impressive, at least to me."

Although he struggled to understand nonverbal clues, the loud groans from those near him would have stopped him had he been sober, but he stood and continued. "Some children can take apart and rebuild a clock they've never seen before, with no help. I can't do that. But even as a child, I could see a business and know how it worked. This Venetian accounting gives me a language to structure what I know. The Venetians have developed…"

The table erupted with, "Double-entry accounting! We know. Shut up, Jakob! Sit down!"

Pelted with bread, he sat down laughing.

Jakob was never rude or mean, but he lacked social skills and was inept with girls; however, he could make money. He missed visual cues and most sarcasm, but he could think through complex transactions with clarity.

Venice's new accounting made it much more difficult for someone to hide profits or losses in the numbers. It didn't make it impossible for a merchant to get screwed over by partners, employees, sellers, or courtiers, but it could reveal who did it and when it happened. Once Jakob understood the fundamentals, he found it elegant. As his Italian accent improved, his accounting improved. As his accounting improved, he grew more confident that he could achieve his mother's goals.

While he enjoyed Venice, he also enjoyed going home. Though the trip took several days, he went home as frequently as he could.

One time, Jakob had returned to Augsburg in time for a huge festival. The Holy Roman Emperor Frederick II was there, and his son Maximilian I took part in the jousts. Frederick II invited Jakob to the emperor's box to watch the joust. He sat under a banner emblazoned with AEIOU, which stood for *Alles Erdisch ist Osterreich Untertan*, All Earth is Under Austria, the emperor's motto. Although, even at 16, Jakob recognized it as wishful thinking rather than reality.

Jakob sat near Frederick, a high honor, and as Frederick accepted a glass of beer from a servant, he lifted his stein and clinked Jakob's glass of red wine. He then called over a stunning girl with beautiful shining hair the color of rich, dark mahogany. She had large brown eyes and a beautiful smile. Frederick told her, "You should see this young man, Jakob Fugger. He will be a man of importance." It was a throwaway compliment, no doubt made as repayment for Jakob's father giving him clothing.

Time froze. Unfortunately, so did Jakob. Jakob barely heard his words as the girl drew his full attention. Far more than simply beautiful, she glowed, with flowing hair hanging past her shoulders.

Slender and graceful, with an elegant neck and bearing, her dark eyes electrified him when she looked at him, and her bright smile took his breath away. He felt as if he were standing near a fire as her warmth flowed over him.

Jakob was so captivated he couldn't speak. He sat still, literally unable to make sounds. The extended silence proved awkward in combination with his obvious enchantment, and the girl returned to her seat, but not before glancing back and winking at Jakob.

He had to leave for Venice late that night. He could not get her out of his mind. Every time he closed his eyes, he saw her. She was much more than pretty. He felt drawn to her as if she were always downhill and being away from her felt painful. She mesmerized him. He barely slept or ate for four days afterward, feverish and entranced. The caravan leader took away the culverin and gave it to a priest because he judged Jakob too dazed to be trusted.

Jakob has dreamed of her since that day.

Back in Venice, it took Jakob a few days to function normally. As their city was built on business, Venetians were more practical in their approach to interest than the more literal, God-fearing Germans. Banks openly paid interest on accounts and invested that money as the bank saw fit. Interest and credit enabled the city to run smoothly and prosper.

By today's standards, it seems ridiculous a teenager could start and run a successful bank, but Jakob did just that. In the fifteenth century, there were no bank regulators, auditors, or stress testers. Anyone with a good name and resources could start a bank. If the founder had money, connections, good credit, and proved trustworthy, the bank would get depositors and lend money.

Jakob accepted deposits and invested in ventures that he felt would have high returns. In part because of his bank, his fascination with accounting, and his crippling inability to speak clearly when near beautiful women, he neither courted nor was he courted. Primarily, however, Jakob was already in love and had little interest in girls other than his winking girl.

Between his bank and several other projects that went well, he earned the nickname "Jakob the Rich." As a banker, Jakob liked the moniker. It cost him nothing, and it gave his depositors assurance that he could pay them back. When his colleagues teased him about the name, he would respond, "It could have been much worse; 'Charles the Fat' was an altogether forgettable French king...except for his name. I could have just as easily been 'Jakob the Awkward.'"

# CHAPTER 11

# LIFE 18.0 -
# THEORIES FLORIDA 2021

After several hours of thought, as he grew hungry for dinner, Jakob called Hartmann. Working in his cage office allowed him to concentrate deeply, despite the persistent smell of copper. It wasn't overpowering at first, but after six or more hours, it felt like someone was shining pennies inches from his nose.

*Once this crisis is resolved, I'll look into getting fresh air piped directly into these offices.*

"Someone has to be spending millions of dollars per week on this mission," Jakob stated. "Keeping teams on-call in major cities across the globe is expensive. Accessing facial recognition systems in real time is expensive. And maintaining the facade required to have police deployed at a moment's notice must be exorbitant."

Hartmann added, "And this has been ongoing for months."

Jakob continued, "I'm unfortunately aware of that. Governments can afford that level of spending, but few individuals can. If it is an individual, they must be wealthy on a governmental scale. Few people are that rich, and none should care about me. So, I have a few theories."

Many billionaires want to delay death and extend their health spans. Bill Gates, Jeff Bezos, and Sergey Brin had each started longevity companies, but their companies focused on biotechnological solutions. They were investigating things like taking drugs to eliminate senescent cells, mitochondrial dysfunction, lengthening telomeres, hyperbaric exposure, Metformin, plasma dilution, and other body-hack solutions.

*But even if one of them wanted me, this isn't their modus operandi. I suspect they would just invite me to Jackson Hole or Davos and try to get me drunk and talking.*

Jakob couldn't talk to Hartmann about the possibility he was being chased because of his immortality, so he focused on his monetary theories. "All of my theories are outlandish, but my first theory is Putin. Estimated to be worth about $200 billion. He says he is worth about $150,000."

Hartmann laughed, "Paparazzi have photographed him dozens of times wearing different Swiss watches that cost more than $150,000."

Jakob replied, "I almost forget you're Swiss, then you say things like that."

Hartmann laughed as Jakob continued. "It isn't impossible that Putin discovered something about my financial situation and now plans to take some of my money for himself. While he isn't the Russian government, he'd have no problem spending government resources to further his agenda. He is unbelievably selfish and a megalomaniac. Even given that, I think the probability of this option is low."

"Hmm, perhaps not that low," responded Hartmann. "What are your other theories?"

"My second theory is that my current nemesis is an oligarch, one of the supremely wealthy Russians that emerged after the fall of the Soviet Union. Several of them have the wealth needed to mount this search even after they gave Putin half in 2005. International bankers refer to those closest to Putin as 'Putin's Wallets,' because they hold so many assets for Putin in their names. It could be one of them. Perhaps they're putting a Putin squeeze on me and others. I think the probability of this option is also low."

"Definitely something to investigate, though," stated Hartmann. Jakob could tell that Hartmann was taking notes by the lags in his response.

"My third theory," Jakob said, "is that it might be a dictator like Kim Jong-un, or Belarus' Alexander Lukashenko, or Iran's Ali Khamenei. North Korea and Iran need money because of their military spending and global sanctions. Belarus is broke too, but that is because Lukashenko has siphoned billions into his own accounts. I know North Korea just prints counterfeit US dollars when it needs cash, but almost everyone knows that now, so maybe it's getting harder for them to spend it. These are all long shots, but they're what I have."

"I'd like to outsource some of the research to some internet specialists," Hartmann replied.

"You mean hackers?" responded Jakob. "Yes. I authorize a budget of $250,000 for them to dig into this, but please have them do it passively. I don't want whoever is after me to know we're after them."

"Got it. Have a nice evening, sir."

"You too, Hartmann," Jakob said, knowing full well that Hartmann and his team would likely work another seven or eight hours.

He walked out into a beautiful night. The humidity had broken and from his back porch, he could see the moon reflecting off the ocean. His Florida house wasn't massive. None of his residences were. Jakob designed them not to draw attention. There were no wings, and none had 30-car garages or basketball courts in the basement. It was a very comfortable 2,600-square foot house. Luxury is in the eye of the beholder, and this house had air conditioning, heat, running water, showers, toilets indoors, comfortable furniture, an excellent bed, and a secure office. Jakob's baseline for extravagance was literally a medieval farmhouse, so a suburban American home felt luxurious to him.

Those with a more discerning eye might notice the Florida house was beachfront and there were no houses on either side for 450 yards. Those undeveloped areas were owned by a wildlife sanctuary charity funded by an anonymous donor that had a peculiar focus on the tracts of land and wildlife around Jakob's homes.

Unique to this house, however, was a set of underground tunnels that Jakob could use to escape to any location, including into the ocean. The tunnel into the surf started behind a locking metal door in his basement, went out about sixty feet past the low tide mark and emerged in a small coral-covered cement room twenty feet underwater. Once in the underwater room, Jakob could activate another tunnel by triggering an air compressor to inflate a submerged tube, 500 yards long and six feet in diameter, that connected to a second submerged room in a marina to the north. Inflating the tube took time, which is why he installed an over-engineered, heavy door. Jakob kept a powerful motorboat docked in that marina on the off chance a water escape became necessary.

As another impractical modification in his Florida house, Jakob had a cellar designed so the chill of the earth and the underground water table kept it at 52 degrees year-round, the perfect temperature for keeping wine. In his cellar, Jakob had a 1990 La Tâche Burgundy that had almost peaked and would spoil soon. He hated the thought of drinking a $10,000 bottle of wine alone, but if he didn't drink it in the next few years, it would turn to vinegar.

*Despite hundreds of years of experience to the contrary, I keep thinking that I will share superb wines with someone special in my life. But that is increasingly unlikely. If I fall in love, I can only love them for a while before not aging is an issue.*

*Nonetheless, hope springs eternal.*

He emerged from the cellar with the Romanée-Conti La Tâche and two glasses; he poured them both and clinked the second glass with his own, then savored the wine as he watched the moonlight dance on the waves and breathed in the air untainted by copper. Jakob sat down in the aqua wrought-iron seat and enjoyed the wine and the night.

# CHAPTER 12

# LIFE 1.0 - SIBYLLE THE PROTESTANT GERMANY 1497

At thirty, Jakob worked with his two surviving brothers, Ulrich and Georg, in Augsburg. The firm was in his brother Ulrich's name, but Jakob didn't care about the name so long as he made the decisions, which he did. The firm prospered, and Jakob flourished but had no male heirs to pass on his legacy.

After fifteen years of working only to build wealth, he thought of marriage. Every time he thought of it, he felt a pit in his stomach as if he were betraying the winking girl. He'd spent years and a lot of money trying to find anything he could about her. She haunted his dreams, and he awoke many mornings yearning for her, but he had no luck in finding out more. The one piece of information one of the "manhunters" he'd hired to find her had discovered, which he felt could be true, was that her name may have been Risacher.

Finding a wife proved challenging for him. He was awkward around men, and nearly catatonic around women. None of Augsburg's single girls seemed interested, whereas their mothers seemed interested (on behalf of their daughters), but Jakob suspected their interest was only because of his wealth. He distrusted anyone that wanted him only for his money.

When he was 38, the wife of the owner of the Augsburg Mint approached Jakob and proposed that Jakob court her daughter, which he did. The daughter, Sibylle, was not impressed by his financial success, which he took as a good sign. Two years later, Jakob married her when she turned 18. The age difference didn't bother Jakob as much as the thought of having to talk regularly with a young woman, particularly one who had no interest in marrying him.

A bright and practical girl, despite her young age, she took her responsibilities as a Grand Burgeress of Augsburg seriously. She had light skin and flowing red hair, which was pretty but felt brittle the few times Jakob touched it. When she smiled, rare though it might be in his company, she could be pretty. She did not like Jakob and soon made him regret the marriage.

Theirs was not one of the new marriages based on love. Love was just being accepted as a reason for marriage in Germania. Jakob brought to the relationship more than enough to support a family, and she brought higher social standing, ergo they married. Neither of them found the other sexually attractive, and they never had children. They never, in fact, got close to having children. For Jakob's part, he couldn't help but compare her to the mesmerizing girl that winked at him, and they slept in separate beds.

The marriage to Sibylle boosted Jakob's social standing, and he became a Grand Burger of the town, which further accelerated his career. They moved into Sybille's mother's house, which he found pleasant as it overlooked the wine market.

Despite his love of making money, he rarely paid attention to material things. He wore clothes of the same cut and dark colors, and the same Venetian-style hat every day. His office was not grand, nor was it even the largest office in the building, though it was the most organized.

But Jakob enjoyed living by the wine market. After decades of drinking beer, he learned to distinguish the wines by their taste and smell, and discovered he favored the pinot noir grapes of Burgundy. His love for pinot noir might have been because he was drinking it when he met the winking girl, or it might have been because it tasted good.

Sibylle matured from a girl to a woman, then progressed to an older woman. She aged. Everyone aged except Jakob. Sibylle hated getting old. She hated her gray hair, wrinkles, and the pains that made small things less enjoyable. Jakob suspected she hated it because she had fallen for one of his business partners, Conrad Railinger. Conrad was a good and likable man, but Jakob could not have him seducing his wife, and he made it clear to both.

As a reward for her grudging fidelity, he built Sibylle the house she wanted. When her mother died, Jakob bought the houses on either side of her mother's and hired architects to combine all three, so Sibylle finally had her mansion.

By the time Jakob turned 60, Sibylle looked noticeably older than him, and one source of his discomfort being around her, aside from her seething dislike of him, had been inverted. Rather than being uncomfortable that he was courting a child, he felt embarrassed that Sibylle looked to be married to a much younger man.

Jakob began to powder his actual hair in the mornings with white. Powdered wigs were coming into fashion in some parts of Europe, but none but Jews powdered their own hair. It was subtle but effective, as he looked older with grayer hair. Unfortunately, every so often, a puff of white would rise from his head if he bumped into someone.

Six years later, after he'd staged his first "death" and moved on to his "second life," Sibylle married Railinger only five weeks after his burial, and then she converted to Protestantism. A religion Jakob feared he'd had a hand in creating.

The aspiring Archbishop Albrecht of Mainz, a man who had purchased three bishoprics, hoped to borrow a great deal of money from Jakob but had no clear path for repayment. In the 1600s, there was no meritocracy of theologians that promoted the most skilled or pious into higher Church offices; instead, those offices went to the highest bidder.

Mainz was the most powerful of the bishoprics because it carried with it the right to elect the Holy Roman Emperor. Controlling the process meant he would receive the largest bribe paid by the new Holy Roman Emperor he elected.

The pope at the time was Leo X, a Medici, who reveled in being pope, but for decidedly non-religious reasons. As an infant, his father bought him his first priesthood, then when he was a teenager, his father bought him a bishopric. When his father then bought him the title of pope, Leo X threw a coronation festival that was wastefully extravagant. Raised wealthy, he enjoyed partying. He partied with absolute abandon and spent all his and all the Vatican's money.

Thus, when it was time to appoint the Archbishop of Mainz, Leo X hinted that his blessing was available for a sizable fortune if that fortune went to himself, not to the Vatican. Albrecht agreed and borrowed the money from Jakob to pay off the pope. Despite his intelligence network telling him Albrecht did not have the assets to repay, Jakob made the loan because Pope Leo X ensured his full repayment. While it was difficult to trust Leo X, it was also politically touchy not to trust him.

Pope Leo X had inherited a construction project from Pope Julius II and had earlier consulted with Jakob on how he might pay for it. He rejected every suggestion about reducing unnecessary expenditures, so Jakob mentioned as an off-handed comment, "You could sell indulgences."

The Vatican had never sold indulgences on that scale. They were used by popes for smaller projects, battles, or to supplement a crusade. This was to be orders of magnitude larger.

However, the idea grew into an ever-larger endeavor as Albrecht and Leo X tried to outdo one another with audacity. Finally, they decided the Vatican would sell indulgences ostensibly to construct a domed marble basilica for St. Peter. It was to be lined with gold and on the massive scale appropriate for an apostle of Jesus. In actuality, some proceeds from the sale of the indulgences would go to the basilica, some would go to Jakob to repay Albrecht's loans, and some would go directly into Leo X's accounts.

St. Peter's indulgences were heavily and grotesquely marketed throughout Germania, promising that the devout could even redeem dead relatives with an indulgence.

"How could you not spend your savings so the mother you loved would avoid the burning torture of purgatory?" friars would demand of the crowds. Further, they claimed these indulgences would cover them for sins they had yet to commit.

Archbishop Albrecht and the pope knew they couldn't sell indulgences in France or Spain because the kings there would demand a cut of the proceeds and enforce it with their armies, so Germania was the easy target because the Holy Roman Emperor had no army to compel a cut.

Albrecht, Leo X, and their indulgence-marketing priests proved very effective at raising funds for St. Peter's Basilica, the Sistine Chapel and the plaza in front of them. The entire process made a mockery of Christianity, but Jakob had long since realized that selfish, self-indulgent men were running the Church and the governments. Although at the time Jakob was a man of strong core beliefs, he was practical, and he accepted a cut of the indulgences as repayment.

Unfortunately for Jakob, the carnival-like sale of St. Peter's indulgences was the proverbial straw that broke the camel's back. A Saxon named Martin Luther finally called the Church out. He made a list of his ninety-five complaints about indulgences and the Church and nailed them to the door of the Wittenberg Cathedral on Halloween, the night before All Saint's Day, a major holy day. He wanted attendees from miles around to see his complaints and see them they did. The Christian world shook from the repercussions.

When he made his protest, Luther had no intention of splitting Christianity into two. He simply wanted the Church to stop the crass marketing of indulgences, priests having sex parties, and buying their Church titles. There were vicious arguments for and against the Vatican.

Protestants emerged protesting the excesses of the Vatican. Never one to pass up an opportunity to enhance his power, England's King Henry VIII, who initially argued against Luther, later changed his mind and created the Protestant Church of England, cutting ties with the pope and putting himself at the head of his new church. Not coincidentally, breaking with the Vatican also helped the king bypass the pope's decision that he couldn't divorce his wife and marry her handmaiden, Anne Boleyn.

The subsequent wars between Catholics and Protestants killed millions of people. The Thirty Years' War alone killed 8 million people. While this number is massive in absolute terms, it is even more horrifying when you realize the population of Germania was only 12 million in the early seventeenth century, and France was not much larger. The equivalent today would be a war that killed 55 million people, three times more Europeans killed than in World War II.

When he was rational, Jakob realized that those wars and deaths came about not because of his expectation of a debt being repaid, but because of a Church that was corrupt to the core, engaging in debauchery while preaching piety, growing wealthy while praising poverty. This holy hypocrisy became more public when syphilis, imported from newly discovered lands in South America, ravaged the Church. Priests, bishops, and popes had their faces and brains eaten away by the sexually transmitted disease.

The Vatican ran the Church like a syndicate for the benefit of the ruling men, not for the benefit of parishioners. Rather than dealing with borrowers who signed their name to a clear contract specifying the exact terms of any loan, the Church misled their flock, stole their money, and abused their trust. Jakob realized religious wars were started by powerful men who wrestled for advantage in a time of turmoil.

The most visible excesses of the Catholic Church were eventually eliminated, but only after millions died. Jakob simply wanted a loan repaid; he didn't want to start religious wars. The deaths of millions of Catholics and Protestants from fighting one another weighed on him every waking moment.

# CHAPTER 13

# LIFE 18.0 -
# ICU FLORIDA 2021

Jakob awoke the next morning with no trace of a headache.

*One of the joys of great pinot noir is you can drink more than you should and still feel good the next morning.*

After cleaning up from a breakfast of four eggs over easy with toast, which he devoured, Jakob walked down to his office and checked the international news sources first, starting with the *Financial Times*. Nothing exciting was happening there. Thinking back on the wine from the night before, Jakob loaded a website, VinsTresBon.com, that sold new-vintage fine wines and older vintage wines with documented provenance. He logged into his account and saw the message icon blinking. He figured it was probably a special offer of an expensive vintage or an offer to sell someone's private wine collection.

*I'll have to check that out in a few minutes after I check the markets.*

Jakob scanned through *The Economist*, *The New York Times*, *The Wall Street Journal*, *The Times*, and the *China Daily*. He made notes of things to check with his family offices.

He planned to go to Italy next. Near La Spezia, on the west coast, there is a village on the Ligurian Sea where he owns a house on the hills. Unlike the nearby Cinque Terre villages and the achingly beautiful town of Porto Venere, the houses and apartments are not brightly colored. Instead, the town is quiet, sunny, and beautiful in its own very ordinary way. There are no tourists. The people that live there either work there or work nearby. But the views are stunning.

Jakob had a potential investment in the area, and he looked forward to driving up to Beaune in France for a day or two of wine tasting in the Burgundy region.

He checked his email and discovered a coded message that informed him Hartmann and his team had been working all night. He called Hartmann. "I would say good morning, but I think your today is a continuation of last night."

Hartmann sounded as alert as if he'd just had a great night's sleep and was all business. "We have ruled out nine of the top twenty Russian oligarchs and categorized eleven others as unlikely."

While there are a hundred oligarchs, only the top twenty could afford to mount a sustained search like the one underway.

Hartmann continued, "We cannot rule out the Putin, Lukashenko, or Kim theories."

"Get some sleep. This may be a long process," said Jakob sympathetically. "I'm going to do some work and maybe that will allow my subconscious to come up with something I've missed."

He made some secure VoIP calls to several of his business associates and investment management teams, which consumed a couple of hours. During one call, Jakob had to recommend they fire the CFO of a biotech company in which his family office was a majority investor. He's had his businesses audited since he was 16 years old in Venice, and his auditors discovered the CFO had been releasing inside information about unannounced R&D products, hoping to drive up the stock price just before her options vested.

*It's too bad; she was an intelligent woman.*

Because of the number of calls, Jakob ate lunch on a call as discreetly as possible and finished with the last call around 2:00 p.m. As he was closing browser windows to shut down the computer, he remembered that he never returned to the VinsTresBon.com wine website, so he opened the message, and the hairs on the back of his neck stood up.

It was a five-letter message.

After turning off his computer, he microwaved the main and backup Mac minis. Jakob grabbed his go-bag, a blue canvas hybrid briefcase/backpack that contained a laptop, chargers, some burner phones, the LED hat, Hartmann's face sparkles, and the blocker, along with Jakob's passports from the US, Portugal and Domenica, a change of clothes, and several currencies. He'd obtained passports from Portugal and Domenica by making legitimate investments in the countries. Jakob headed calmly for his ocean exit.

In the tunnel, as he walked under the ocean, Jakob called Hartmann on WhatsApp, waking him up, and told him what happened. Ever since Facebook had purchased Whatsapp, Jakob stopped using its text messaging, but every sign was that its voice product was still secure. He asked Hartmann to double the spend on hackers and access the wine website server and their ISP to find out who left the message.

Jakob also called his concierge service and told them he would be going to his house in Italy, requesting that they have it cleaned and stocked. He also asked them to buy him a business-class ticket to Nice, France, and rent a car for the drive to La Spezia.

He made one more call as he processed the conflicting rush of emotions.

*On one hand, I've lived over five centuries and would prefer not to break that streak. But, on the other hand, my life just got even more interesting.*

As he walked through the pressurized underwater tube towards his boat, he could still see the email message in his mind's eye:

**JF ICU**

# CHAPTER 14

# LIFE 1.0 -
# THE BARMAID AUGSBURG 1499

J akob did not have many friends. He didn't have much to talk about with other men. Focused primarily on business, he also enjoyed reading and talking about the few history books he could find. Jakob enjoyed talking about foreign lands, and what was happening in the courts of kings and princes. For hours, he could talk about commerce.

However, it seemed to Jakob that the men of Augsburg primarily talked of jousts, drinking, how drunk they'd been, how much they hated work, how shitty the weather was, and of whoring. None of it interested Jakob. By the time he had turned 25, he was among the wealthiest men in Augsburg, and this made friendships even more awkward. In part, he didn't enjoy spending time the way many men did. He worked six days a week and twelve hours a day, and enjoyed it.

After thinking he was making real friends, those friends asked for money, which made him suspicious of their friendship. He feared none of these were the primary reason he didn't have friends. When he was honest with himself, he admitted he didn't have friends because he didn't know how to.

Jakob had even less success with women or girls. The prettier they were, the more tongue-tied and less coordinated he became around them. He struggled to look anyone in the eyes when he talked to them, and with women, it was much more challenging. He knew the words used to flatter women, but words were only successful if Jakob could keep them interested, a skill he found elusive. Few women liked to talk about business. Further, the suspicion he had of potential male friends liking him only for money doubled with women.

Jakob had tried whoring, but found it gave him the same feeling he got when he ate a splendid meal that had grown cold and sour. His lack of social skills left him lonely, but he grew used to that. An emotional callus built up over time. He had internalized his mother's goal of making a lot of money, and he was good at it. He told himself he needed nothing more.

However, Jakob did like the arts. He still hungered to learn about the world, and he hired tutors to improve his language skills and to teach him about places he hadn't visited. But his most successful interactions with his peers became transactional.

There was one exception. Jakob befriended Adelle, a barmaid in the main Augsburg tavern. Her head was enormous, and she was shaped like a barrel with slim legs protruding from the bottom of the barrel. She had poor teeth and facial warts. But she was very smart, and she was funny.

He'd known her as a teen, but he really met her when he was twenty-six and overheard her speaking French with some travelers, suggesting they avoid the particular white wine they were contemplating if they planned to get out of bed the next day. As she walked near his corner table, giving him the nod they'd exchanged for years, Jakob said in French that her accent was superb. Jakob discovered that, like him, she spoke several languages.

From that point on that evening, they spoke in languages other than German. She would say something in Spanish, and Jakob would reply in Italian. She'd ask if he wanted anything more to drink in Netherland Dutch, and he'd order another wine in English. They became fast friends.

On slow nights, she would join him at his corner table and talk about life, travel, religion, and business. When she first arrived in Augsburg thirty years before, she had talked her way into being a barmaid despite not looking the part. Her memory was astounding. She didn't get orders wrong, and she controlled the patrons with a biting wit. They talked about books and how Gutenberg's press had changed more than just religious texts. Jakob learned she had quietly acquired the tavern and two of the adjoining buildings over the years she worked there.

Years later, she admitted she felt like a failure because she'd never married, and Jakob pointed out it may be too late to have children, but not to marry. "Find a pretty man and make him your house husband."

She laughed aloud at that thought. "I'd have him bring me meals in bed and rub my aching feet! He'd peel my grapes and fan me in the summer heat."

Jakob eventually admitted to his trouble befriending most people, and she told him of her brother, a musical savant, who was painfully awkward around others but could play any instrument. That planted the idea that perhaps Jakob was a commerce savant.

One night, years later, he asked her why she was so private about being the owner of the tavern.

She explained, "Nobody needs to know my business. It took me years to tell you and you're my genuine friend. I tell you because I know you aren't out to do me any harm, but who knows about others? A woman today has few defenses for success and fewer rights, so anyone who wants to know my private business is likely out to take something I have."

She flipped the conversation. "So...your turn. I know you are wealthier than most princes by now, yet you live simply. Why?"

"Essentially," he replied after some thought, "for the same reasons. Through my bank, I lend money for interest. The church could condemn me for usury, and I'd have to waste time and money defending myself, and still might lose everything. So, I keep how much I have private. To most people, I want to appear wealthy enough to be a legitimate banker. I don't need more horses, a castle, or fancier clothes. I prefer to avoid unnecessary attention."

She lifted her stein. "To avoiding unnecessary attention!"

Jakob lifted his glass of pinot noir. "Prost!"

Adelle was the only person, aside from his wife, who knew that he didn't seem to age. In her sixties, she found it splendid. But he felt less sure.

When tipsy one night, he admitted to her, "One big reason I don't want anyone to know is because others might perceive it as the work of Satan." Jakob, a Catholic, believed for most of his early life that Satan was as real as horses. He further admitted, "And I fear they might be right."

She laughed at that, spraying the floor and Jakob's legs with beer. "If Satan was working through you, he'd rot your crotch, not make you stay young, rich, and healthy. Sorry about the beer."

She was very smart.

A cold November night well after sunset, he came into the tavern and took his usual table. She pulled a bottle from France's Burgundy region from behind her bar, and as the cold kept most patrons at home, she sat down and joined him with two glasses.

"So tell me," she said as she poured the wine, "success in commerce seems to be easy for you. Why do you work so hard?"

"An ironic question coming from someone that works longer hours than I do," Jakob replied.

She nodded, conceding his point, but pressed on: "Seriously, why?"

Jakob thought for a minute, then said, "First, let me clarify. Almost none of the projects I work on turn out just as I'd hoped, so I change my approach and adjust until I find a way to make them pay off.

"Because I'd earned enough by the age of twenty-five, very few projects I undertake put me at risk of not eating. Others engage in commerce and borrow to do it, so they can afford to have only one or two things go wrong before their loan is called. I am my own lender in most cases and have the luxury of both time and money. Those are the luxuries I like most.

"But, as to why I work. I feel if you are going to work hard with the goal of getting wealthy, which I admit is not everyone's goal, doing something that you enjoy, pays well, and doesn't hurt others, is as good as it gets.

"It's an extra benefit if it helps others somehow, but even if it doesn't, that does not mean that I can't help them later. As a child, my mother's dream was for me to be rich enough to deal with princes, emperors, and the pope. As a boy, those men seemed magical in their power and brilliant, but now I work with them all the time, and they are just people filled with the same petty fears and jealousies as everyone else. So, I keep building to help people who don't knowingly ruin their own lives and those of their children. That's why I had the Fuggerai built to house workers, not the indolent. Even though the rent is almost nothing, you must have a job to live there."

"Fair points," she said, "but when do you stop?"

"When I die," he answered. "If I die," he whispered jokingly, but Adelle didn't laugh.

Jakob continued, "I have worked for decades to create an organization that generates income and wealth. I've built several businesses and enjoyed doing it. Aside from the financial rewards, I most enjoy the process of envisioning something that doesn't exist and motivating myself and others to create it. I build things out of air, with just self-discipline and dedication of resources. I've created these mines, banks, smelting facilities, and other businesses while maintaining my integrity and striving to be fair to everyone with whom I work. Why would I stop?"

Adelle realized the question was rhetorical, which Jakob appreciated. They finished the bottle.

# CHAPTER 15

# LIFE 18.0 - BLACKFEET NATION MONTANA 2021

The commercial plane flew in a holding pattern before it could land, and Jakob's paranoia made him question whether it was because of him or just standard airport delays. He could do little about it now because even his security team didn't know he was coming to Montana. However, the delay did give him a chance to see the beautiful Montana mountains and Flathead Lake from the air.

Jakob had always worked to be prepared for things to go wrong, and now he was particularly pleased that he'd thought of establishing the relationship that was about to prove very helpful. His German thriftiness made him feel bad that airline tickets to Nice would go unclaimed, and a week's worth of groceries would be thrown away when he didn't show up at his Italian house. But the JF ICU message had him spooked, and he wanted to throw his pursuers off the trail.

In his previous life, roughly forty years before, Jakob established a relationship with the Blackfeet Nation and was granted honorary Blackfeet status. Jakob never claimed he was a Native American and it was clear in looking at him he wasn't, but he was allowed to choose a Blackfeet name. Not one to let a pun slip by, he took the Blackfeet name John Many Holes, and spoke occasionally of his son, Jakob.

As John Many Holes, he had also earned rights to establish a small ranch on the reservation fronting Lower Saint Mary Lake, which is stunning at sunset.

In his last life, 17.0, the plight of American Indians particularly bothered Jakob, specifically those on reservations. They were poor, and the reservations were a mess, partially because the American government gave the Indians awful real estate. But Jakob didn't work to befriend the Blackfeet just to revel in cultural appropriation. Instead, he saw a need he could help with.

It exacerbated the problems on the reservations if Native Americans with ambition left the reservation and didn't come back. Though not politically correct, Jakob believed a tribal decision hindered prosperity because individuals could not own land. Only the tribe has a legal claim to the land.

For most other Americans, much of their net worth was in real estate. However, without a clear land title, many Native Americans can't get a mortgage, and it made little sense to sink money into home improvements because the land was the tribe's. Also, nontribal banks were wary of lending for reservation real estate because they had limited recourse and were dependent on tribal police to enforce any court orders.

Jakob believed this was why mobile homes were so prevalent on reservations. If the tribe decided you needed to move, you could move your house in a few hours. Mortgages were rare on the reservation, and houses paid for in cash tended to be inexpensive. A century or five of racism didn't help the economic situation much either. For a myriad of reasons, Native Americans were deeply impoverished.

Jakob can't sing, he's a terrible poet, not very athletic, and he's the only one who believes he's a good dancer, but it turns out Jakob had a skill set that allows him to look at a situation and figure out how to make money from it. His solution to reducing Indian poverty was the Indian Gaming Regulatory Act. Of course, casinos come with their own problems, but casinos make a lot of money!

When he first started building on the reservation, as John Many Holes, all Blackfeet did not accept him. He nearly died because a gang, who were drunk and high on peyote, thought he was just another white invader. That night, while on the reservation to oversee construction of his log cabin, he heard motorcycles revving around the lake and wasn't concerned. But when the windows of his almost-finished cabin started shattering as rocks flew through them, he got nervous.

He called his security team, which was about an hour away, but wasn't able to say much before the line went dead. The Indians on their iron horses, as they called them, had surrounded his cabin. Two of them dragged him outside, then the group pushed him around, not hurting him. It took Jakob a while to realize they were planning to hang him.

They forced him to stand on the seat of an idling Harley Davidson adorned with fringe on the handlebars and saddlebags, its kickstand in the dirt. He had to stand very straight not to tighten the noose around his neck. Even idling, the Harley seemed to shake itself apart. The mob danced and chanted around him, weaving from the drugs, and drunk from whatever they'd been drinking and the excitement of screwing around with a white invader.

*I don't know if I will die if they hang me, but I don't plan to find out.*

As John Many Holes, he began to yell out. "When the reservations were established, the US government didn't want Indians on the reservations to get quite the same benefits as other Americans."

They slowed only slightly, but a few looked up at him. He continued yelling, "Each tribal nation has its own government, can make its own rules, and decide what to do on its land."

One warrior, who wore an auto repair shop shirt that identified him as Tony, yelled up at him, "We know this, Áápi Imitáá. That's why you will die tonight." Tony's claim seemed as if it might indeed happen. Smoke from the idling motorcycle was making Jakob dizzy, and the rope cut into his neck. His feet were cramping from keeping him balanced.

*"Ayoohtsiwa Nínaa!"* Jakob screamed back in Siksika. "Listen, man!"

His Siksika, the language of the Blackfeet, was limited, and his pronunciation poor, but it had an immediate effect. They all stopped, stunned. Tony, who had moments before been the most eager to kill him, said, "Let him speak."

"Thank you," Jakob said, regaining his balance after yelling. "The US government didn't think it through! You have a nation. A nation! You set your own laws on your lands. In the regular USA, nowhere except in Las Vegas can people gamble, so Las Vegas rakes in billions of dollars alone. Detroit can't allow casinos because the US government says so, neither can Wichita, but the Blackfeet reservation..."

By this point, one of them moved to untie the rope from around the trunk of the tree. Tony, now smiling, interrupted Jakob, "But the

Blackfeet reservation doesn't have those same rules, because it is its own nation!"

"Exactly," Jakob said, gingerly lifting the rope from around his neck and rubbing the chafed skin under it. "I am confident the Blackfeet can partner with the other tribal nations and flip the government's rules on their asses. You can start to get some of the casino money. You can do things that non-Indians can't, and you may as well make money from it!"

"Hell yeah!" one of the warriors yelled as he started stomping a double-tap warrior dance. He stopped a moment later, sheepishly, when nobody joined him.

"Why do we need you?" Tony asked. It was a reasonable question.

Jakob was honest. "You don't need me, but I'm rich and good at this stuff. It is an idea I can help make a reality, and we can get the gambling licenses in three years if we work together. In three years, you can be rich, not just a bit less poor. Florida and California tribes already have bingo on reservations and, without me, I'm sure you can get bingo here in several years, and maybe you'll get a few dollars each."

Tony came over and held the Harley as Jakob stepped down. "I'd like to be rich in three years."

"Then let's work together because I'd like to make you rich in three years," Jakob replied, shaking Tony's hand.

The group sat around a huge bonfire and shared too many of Jakob's finer bottles of wine that night as he laid out his strategy. At one point, Jakob got up to go to the bathroom. Rather than pee in his own front yard, he walked into his now windowless house and saw one of his security team standing where Jakob could see him, but the gang outside couldn't.

Startled, Jakob asked, "How long have you been here?"

"We got here just as you started yelling in Siksika, but you seemed to get the shit show under control, so we stayed hidden," he responded. "Can you really do what you said to help the tribe?"

"Yes, I can."

"That's outstanding!" he whispered. "We'll disappear."

"Thank you," Jakob replied.

"Thank *you*," the man replied, hugging Jakob suddenly. "My name is Thomas Brown Claw. Call me if you ever need help." Then he left and three men who had been invisibly standing in the shadows silently filed out behind him.

Tony became an ambassador to the other tribes and, after visiting and convincing thirty of them to work with the Blackfeet team, the remaining 150 tribes visited him and requested to join in. After three years of invisible effort on Jakob's part and hard work on the part of many others, including Tony and Thomas Brown Claw, American Indians could legally operate casinos on their land. Casinos came with their own problems. But casinos make a lot of money!

Now, while on the reservation, Jakob had the protection of tribal law. As an adjunct member of the Tribal Business Council and a friend of Earl Old Person, the honorary chief of the tribe, Jakob had raised several million dollars in donations for the reservation to install a fiber-optic network. It is possible that his fundraising may have helped establish his friendship with the tribe more quickly than was likely from Jakob's witty repartee alone.

The jolt of the airplane's wheels hitting the runway brought Jakob out of his musings and back to the present.

*There is more I can do, but I need time to implement. The one thing I have in abundance is time—unless this "JF ICU" thing proves fatal.*

The taxi dropped Jakob off at the reservation entrance, and the security guard recognized him because he'd worked with her father. He walked onto the reservation and found his truck where he'd parked it months ago. A solar panel that plugged into the lighter outlet kept the battery charged, and it started right up. Jakob's place wasn't far from the western entrance.

He pulled up to his ranch and parked the pickup truck in the shade of trees he'd planted for just that purpose as John Two Holes, forty years before. He exited the truck and walked to the door wearing mirrored sunglasses and a cowboy hat with a large feather given to him by the elders, which he kept in the truck.

The hat provided protection, if not by channeling protective spirits as promised, then at least by shielding him from being identified by any of his pursuers' drones that might be overhead. A biometric lock would have stood out, so the cabin was only secured by a hook and eyelet on the screen door. Only the door to the basement and the wine cellar was biometrically locked. A gray and brown blanket covered the scanner; after forty years, it still left his fingers smelling like a wet horse after he moved it to the side.

Once inside the cabin, Jakob moved to the basement door. After the retinal scan and a waft of horse scent, the door swung open. After descending into his office, Jakob took out his phone and reviewed the list of to-do items he'd composed in airplane mode on the flight. Looking at his list, he could hear his mother's voice: "If it is important, write it down. If you don't write it down, it isn't important to you."

His password manager somehow could tell he was in a hurry and so made him enter his master password three times just to be frustrating.

First on the list was to check in with Hartmann, which Jakob did, and found an email. Decrypting it took his computer about a minute. While it worked, Jakob went upstairs and made himself a peanut butter sandwich after toasting bread he'd left in the freezer.

Hello Sir. We breached the wine server, and found the message was placed four days ago from an Internet cafe in a small south German town, Augsburg. Our subcontractors scanned everything on the server and ISP and found nothing malicious. One odd thing though, six cases of Romanée-Conti were shipped to Maximilianstraße in Augsburg six months prior. No name was listed on the account, and they paid in cash.

I suggest you go to the mattresses until we know more.

Jakob had to smile at the *Godfather* reference. In preparation for a Mafia gang war, the men would leave their homes and families and go to a safe house, sleeping on mattresses on the floor.

*Augsburg is a surprising twist.*

Jakob had lived on Maximilianstraße, Maximilian Street, back when it was the wine market in Life 1.0. He built his wife a mansion there. The burgundy was also odd. Romanée-Conti costs at least €2,500 per bottle, or US $2,860, so someone had just spent about US $210,000 cash on one order of wine.

*The coincidences are getting very weird, although I think that it may not result in my death. Until I know more, I can't drop my guard.*

Jakob felt safer on the reservation than in Florida or Virginia. It wasn't only with gambling where tribal law overrode state and local law. It was on all legal matters. State or local agents cannot make arrests on reservations, they can only petition the tribal police to do so on their behalf, but the tribal police decide if they want to pursue it. Jakob had recently made generous donations to the current Blackfeet Tribal Chief of Police's election and bought her department five police-ready Dodge Challengers. The cars were impractical in the desert but much coveted by the officers, and so it seemed unlikely that she would rush to comply with an outside request involving Jakob.

*Even with the added layer of protection, I cannot relax.*

Second on his list was a reminder to send up drones of his own. The drones took some time as he had to launch each independently and set up charging stations on the roof of his back porch so they could return to base and recharge. When he started, he figured it would take him an hour. But after three hours of drone setup and an hour of horrendously bad drone flying on his part, Jakob finally had a grid of six views established: the front of the ranch, the road in, the lake, the entrance to the reservation, and two random search patterns, all displayed on the 55" flat screen tv in his living room.

Third on the list was for him to get Hartmann in contact with his European security team. From his office, Jakob connected with Hartmann, then conferenced-in Bernthaler in Munich.

After introductions, Hartmann started the call with an efficient review of the situation and what his team found. When he finished, Jakob asked Bernthaler to determine who ordered the burgundy cases and to trace who had hacked into the wine website to leave him the message. Jakob told them both that he would continue to puzzle out the meaning of "JF ICU," but until they knew better, the default assumption was that JF was himself, and ICU meant, "I see you," and they should treat it as a threat. The only new information from Hartmann was that his team determined it was very unlikely that his pursuer came from North Korea.

CHAPTER 16

# LIFE 1.0 -
# SPOILED CHILDREN HUNGARY 1515

J akob had an attractive investment opportunity in Hungary. Although he already owned several silver and copper mines, Hungary had mines rich in copper that he'd wanted for years, and they were available at last. Copper was in high demand because mixing copper and zinc made brass and brass was popular. Hungary's shared border with the Turks made the deal complicated.

In 1515, the Ottoman Empire, sometimes called the Turkish Empire, was already larger than France and Spain combined, and was expanding. Jakob's existing copper mines in Hungary, his smelting factories, and the additional mines he wanted to control would be easy pickings for the Turks because the Hungarian King Ladislaus could not mount a sufficient defense if the Turks mounted a large attack.

The unprotected border put his copper and silver at imminent risk, and the Turks had been conducting more and bolder slaving incursions, capturing young girls in Hungarian territory.

The Turks did not like Christians, whom they viewed as infidels. They disliked Germans and Austrians with a vengeance. They hated the Hungarians, given that a Transylvanian count, Vlad Dracula, left a vivid national memory for the Turks with his savage display of hundreds of Turkish heads impaled on stakes. Further, Sharia law forbade interest, so the Turks detested moneylenders. The Turks, therefore, were unlikely to find Jakob loveable.

To make matters worse, the Hungarian peasants were also a threat to the mines. Unable to afford a professional army, Hungarian King Ladislaus had attempted to raise and train a peasant army to fight off the Turks. However, once they got arms, the peasants turned on the Hungarian nobility. Their anger at the nobility proved more intense than their anger at the Turks, despite the Turks abducting girls.

At 56, Jakob had grown tired of kings creating problems for themselves, their subjects, and him by making childish decisions. Jakob had spent decades nudging kings, princes, bishops, and popes towards rational decisions. His mother would have been proud, but Jakob was getting exhausted. When younger, he didn't mind lending to someone so they could pursue a folly if he made money on the transaction. Jakob, through rational decisions, had become wealthier than most of the kings of Europe. With that wealth came influence.

Jakob realized his wealth was a double-edged sword. It was impressive to some; it seemed terribly selfish to others. And everyone coveted it. Capitalism and rational thinking were just taking hold in Europe. Jakob understood how to make money, but almost nobody else at the time did, so it wasn't a fair competition. His marriage was a farce. He had no children and no heirs, so he continued doing what he enjoyed and did best.

To make his purchase of the mines pay off, Jakob knew he had to secure them. Although quite charming, the Holy Roman Emperor

Maximilian did not have a long attention span. He had, in theory, agreed to help the Hungarians, but he became distracted time after time and didn't follow through. The Hungarian king, Ladislaus, had a group of armed peasants trying to overthrow him, and desperately wanted an alliance with Maximilian, but couldn't get him to focus. Jakob wanted to keep the Turks out of Hungary; using captured girls as slaves offended him deeply, and he wanted his mines to be secure.

Getting the emperor and the king together was the key to solving his problem. After several glasses of wine, Jakob wrote to Maximilian and told him that if he ever wanted another florin, he would meet with Ladislaus and come to an agreement that would put Hungary under the Hapsburgs' protection. Quite to Jakob's surprise, it worked.

The two met and, for reasons he would never understand, they included the cunning King Sigismund of Poland. The meeting went superbly. To Jakob's amazement, Poland somehow got Prussia out of the deal, but Maximilian and Ladislaus announced a double wedding tying their families together. Given it was a royal wedding in the sixteenth century, two of the betrothed were children. Maximilian's grandson would marry Ladislaus' daughter. She was 11 and several years older than her groom. The marriages would protect Hungary from the Turks, discourage the peasants from any further attempts at a coup, and secure Jakob's mines.

Jakob celebrated the outcome. Not as much as the Polish king, however, who made out better than anyone else.

Jakob looked at good business as an art form. If he were a skilled artist, it seemed unlikely that people would expect him to stop painting because he'd painted enough masterpieces. But he was constantly asked why he didn't stop making money. Even among educated people and the nobility, there was a perception that Jakob was taking it from someone else.

Months after their weddings were announced, Jakob was cornered by an Austrian princess, dressed head to toe in pink, at a banquet for her father.

"Thank you, Herr Fugger, for helping end the Turkish raids. I suspect it was an incidental benefit for you to secure the mines you wanted, but thank you anyway. I have asked around about you, and I hear you are richer than kings, yet you still dedicate yourself to commerce. Why is that?"

He responded at length, "I am so very pleased the slaving raids have ended. But to answer your question directly, I enjoy my work. By establishing and growing commerce, I am increasing the wealth of Europe, not taking money from someone else. Historically, if a king wanted something, he went to war and took it, killing thousands and ruining many more lives.

"Except for indulgences, I have always traded something to get something back, and both parties walked away with what they wanted. But perhaps I'm wrong about indulgences. Maybe the pope's scrolls indeed are pulling tortured souls out of purgatory."

The pink princess' eyes went wide. Jakob had just blasphemed by questioning the pope's sale of indulgences. Further, Jakob suspected she started the conversation expecting to engage in some courtly flirtation, rich with double entendre and clever wordplay, but light on substance. Yet she knew about the mines, so she wasn't without an understanding of commerce.

So, he continued, "It takes a different eye to see my businesses as things of beauty, but I find them beautiful. I employ hundreds of thousands of people and help feed their families. Their wages allow them to build warm homes. I pay them fair wages. And I teach them skills."

She recovered enough to respond with a whisper, "But dear Jakob, they work in mines."

He responded with a nod and a small smile, "Not all work in mines. Working in a mine doesn't sound like a desirable lifestyle, but you recall that these men were subsistence farmers before working in a mine. I grew up on a farm. Farming for a living is brutal, deadly, and rarely done well. If a farmer has ten children, six or seven die young, and so do the farmer and his wife. Working in one of my mines is an improvement over subsistence farming."

She raised an eyebrow at that, engaged but skeptical.

Jakob went on, "I have irrefutable proof. Four or five men fight, literally punching one another, for each available job when my mines announce they are hiring. People who are looking to improve their lives don't fight to get jobs worse than their current jobs.

"Further, by lending money, I help the economy grow. An economy with no credit is limited to slow or no growth. In your great-grandfather's time, there was little credit and there was little growth. Your father borrowed from me and has grown his lands tenfold with no war, no death, and no maimed soldiers. He didn't lie or steal, instead made fair deals and invested wisely. His financial improvement allows his lovely daughter to dress herself with such…flair."

She nodded and placed a hand on Jakob's arm. "You make good points."

Conspiratorially, Jakob bent to whisper in her ear, "But I must admit that I look forward to stopping what I'm doing with this group

95

of selfish children. My parents would never have imagined anyone, much less me, calling the Holy Roman Emperor, the pope, and the kings of countries spoiled children and meaning it. But there it is."

His pink-clad friend then gave a gasp of surprise, raised her glass of wine, and touched it to his glass before she, in a very unladylike fashion, downed the whole glass.

He had far surpassed his father's goals; he'd even surpassed his mother's goals and found life pursuing wealth hollow. So, he decided he would work while he enjoyed working, and when he stopped enjoying it, he'd do something different. He did not know what that would be, but he gave it serious consideration.

He didn't know that he would live for centuries. All he knew was that, without the hair powder, he looked and felt 35 despite being twenty-five years older than that. He realized that if he would not die soon of natural causes, which was looking less likely each year, he might want to "die" a different way. Like a phoenix, he could then rise from the ashes as another person.

He found the thought so appealing that he had even decided on a new name. "Two Holes" was Jakob's favorite brother, the one his sister had stabbed in the rear. In his honor, Jakob had determined to become Jakob Lochzwei, or in English, Jakob Holestwo.

His companies' tight accounting and audits would make his next steps more challenging. All of his bookkeepers used double-entry accounting, and he had the companies audited. Jakob determined to take a fraction of his wealth and set it aside, so that he could access it as Jakob Lochzwei if needed.

With no children of his own, he chose his nephews to run the businesses after his death. His nephews worked for him already, but he created a board of advisors to bring them into his confidence, at least concerning the businesses. They learned about the company's physical assets, the mines, the smelting businesses, and they grew to understand the bank and its criteria for lending. The nephews visited regional offices and performed audits. Jakob explained the personalities of the players and which few were trustworthy. He also sold one of the Hungarian mines to a company owned by a new entrant into the mining business, Herr Lochzwei.

Over the next several years, there were threats of wars, there were actual wars, and great intrigue in the courts of Europe. Governments seized Jakob's properties and then released them. He made successful investments and ones that disappointed, but overall, he grew the businesses significantly.

At one point, after having avoided it for decades, he was charged with the religious crime of usury. This put all his companies in jeopardy. He had spent his life carefully avoiding a usury charge, but one of his debtors believed calling him out for usury would cause the debt to be dismissed. A significant donation to the pope led him to a religious epiphany, and he declared that charging interest was no longer a sin. The man who had charged Jakob with usury found himself evicted from the estate he had pledged as collateral, and unable to borrow again.

With utmost discretion, Jakob set up the life of Herr Lochzwei, and it was going better than expected. Some proceeds were flowing into an account in Hamburg's Berenberg Bank, where they would stay, and compound, until he needed them.

Jakob began to look for opportunities to "die." Over time, he developed a plan. Given his slowed aging, he speculated he might live to 90 or 100, an age almost unheard of when most adults died in their forties. He had no idea he'd live far beyond that.

In his next "life," Jakob did not plan to focus on growing wealth for himself. For even with the fraction he'd set aside, he would have more than he could ever spend. Instead, he wanted to make up for his part in starting the Catholic-Protestant religious wars and causing all the pointless deaths.

As Christmas approached in 1525, to all appearances, Jakob fell ill, and he revised his will. He named his two surviving nephews to run the companies and gave a small gift to each of the inhabitants in the Fuggerai, the affordable housing complex he had built for the working poor in Augsburg. He parceled out generous, but not ruinous, amounts to nieces and nephews and gave his most valued business associates amounts that would last them a lifetime.

A few years prior, rumors had circulated that Jakob had fathered a daughter with a prostitute just before his marriage. He knew this wasn't true, but went to see his alleged daughter, who worked as a maid in a large Augsburg home. He discovered the speculation that Jakob was the father was deemed credible because she was good at math, as was Jakob. Such was the poor logic of the day that most people didn't question the rumor.

Jakob discovered her to be exceptionally good at math, much better than many of his managers, and so hired her to oversee some of his investments, launching another scandal. Jakob left her an inheritance that allowed her to purchase the home she'd cleaned in Augsburg and retire in comfort. The rumors died down once people saw them together as she was quite swarthy, almost twice his size and the two looked nothing alike.

His wife, Sibylle, had begun an affair with Conrad Railinger, a breach of trust which made Jakob much sadder than he would have ever guessed. She had apparently been staying slender from the misery of staying true to Jakob, but since beginning her affair, she'd doubled her weight. Although he felt petty at the thought, he wondered if her ballooning size was God's revenge for her infidelity. The affair was also a breach of the explicit agreement the two had made that if she remained faithful, she would have a mansion in Augsburg. He had built her a mansion covering a city block in Augsburg, but she did not stay faithful, so she did not get the mansion in his will.

The night before New Year's Eve in 1525, it was announced that Jakob had died. Two well-trusted servants attending him at the time brought in a body similar in size and shape to Jakob's that they had located the day before. They dressed the poor man in Jakob's clothing, shaved him, cut and powdered his hair, and placed Jakob's hat on the corpse's head. He looked like a dead Jakob, or close enough. They then shrouded him as the corpse, and after Jakob gave each of his death assistants 500 florins—a fortune—with a promise of 500 florins per year for the next nine years if they never spoke of it, Jakob Lochzwei left through the servants' quarters, eager to begin his new life in a new year.

# CHAPTER 17

# LIFE 18.0 -
# SUNSET MONTANA 2021

O n his fifth day in Montana, Jakob's computer alarm went off, drawing him out of the rabbit hole of reports from his family office. While he didn't attend investor meetings of the private equity funds he had invested in, as a favor, they sent him the deal memos.

The term "memo" is a misnomer because it implies perhaps two or three pages. However, before family offices or private equity funds invest huge amounts, they pull together dense and comprehensive reports on the company in which they want to invest. They can run to hundreds of pages; they kept Jakob abreast of different industries much better than trade magazines or investment bank reports, but they were not light reading.

Jakob reached into the drawer near his desk and pulled out a pre-paid smartphone. There were several in the drawer.

*It may be overkill, but I'm not taking any chances now.*

When possible, he tried to watch the sunset, so he closed down his computers, let himself out of his office cage, and headed up to the front porch for fresh air. The house was a "full round" log cabin, made from logs longer and wider than modern telephone poles. It was an oddity on the reservation because it was immovable, with a large wrap-around porch that overlooked the lake to the west. As he walked through the family room with a glass of wine in hand, he glanced up at the drone feeds. There were two vehicles just outside the reservation entrance.

*It is not alarming, but it's odd to see any traffic there. I will check back on that.*

The sunset was glorious. Pinks, oranges, and golds highlighted the clouds and reflected off the water. Years before, Hartmann had set up a microcell for wireless voice and data spoofed so it appeared to be connecting through Port Clinton, Ohio. Removing the plastic packaging from the cell phone was much more challenging than getting the phone set up and semi-secure by installing NordVPN, Tor Browser, and WhatsApp. Once the phone was ready, Jakob WhatsApp'd Hartmann.

"Hello, sir," Hartmann said.

"Hi," replied Jakob. They didn't use names on WhatsApp, secure or not. "I want to run something by you. I want to reply to the wine message taking all precautions, using Tor over a VPN on a burner phone over the Montana wireless data network. Can you be ready to sniff any traffic?"

Hartmann said nothing for about four minutes, but Jakob could hear furious typing and hushed conversations in the background. Then he responded, "All set."

Jakob launched the virtual private network software and selected a server in Germany. Next, he launched the Tor Browser and logged into the wine company's site. He opened his notifications again and there was the message.

**JF ICU**

Jakob typed a simple message back.

**Who RU?**

Then he disconnected, removed the battery, and ground the SIM card under his boots. He tried to break the phone like he'd seen in spy movies and realized why the movies use flip phones for burners.

*I can't twist this thing apart without tools, maybe even heavy machinery.*

Jakob had finished his glass of wine, so he sat back and watched the sky slowly fade to gray. Apologizing to the lake, he stepped to the edge of his porch and side-armed the undamaged phone into the water. It skipped eight times before it sank.

*Now is when I'd really like to have someone around to see things like that. Eight skips with a phone!*

He walked back inside to make some dinner, refill his wine glass, and throw away the burner's battery. As he walked past his cowboy hat, he smiled to himself. In Europe, as he heard the stories and read the pamphlets about America's Wild West in the mid-1800s, he never thought that one day he'd have a log cabin in the West and be wearing a cowboy hat.

*It has been an amazing experience to have had so many different lives in different places.*

Because he couldn't have his concierge service stock the house before he arrived without tipping his trackers, Jakob's cuisine choices were steak or steak. He'd pulled one out of the freezer hours before and by dusk, the steak had thawed, so Jakob turned on the gas burner and brought out a cast-iron skillet. The wine tasted great, and he made a mental note to save some to drink with the steak. To complete the full cowboy lifestyle, he also had canned beans.

Jakob walked slowly up the slope as the mist cleared. The bodies were everywhere, some mangled, others whole, but their stench of decay was everywhere. He never saw them move, but their dead eyes were always on him. As he crested the hill, he looked down at tens of thousands of bodies. All of them accused him with their eyes.

He awoke coated in sweat. Climbing out of bed, he knew he wouldn't sleep any more that night. He hated that dream but knew it was one of God's punishments for his role in the religious wars. In Big Sky country, the sun was already rising, and as Jakob walked into the main room, he stopped dead.

On the TV above the fireplace, he saw there were now several cars at the reservation entrance. Two tribal police SUVs and a police Dodge Challenger were on the tribal land inside the gate. The last vehicle in the line outside the reservation was a big pickup pulling what looked like a three-horse carrier. As Jakob watched, a man walked an already saddled horse off the back of it.

*Whoever they are, they aren't driving in the entrance of the reservation with the tribal police on this side. That means that they aren't operating under federal authority, so it was most likely state. But once they're on horseback, jurisdiction won't matter. I'm certain they will find a way to cross onto the reservation. Once again, it is time to go.*

He didn't worry about the computers downstairs. If someone breached the door without his biometrics, a switch would activate a high-powered magnet that would scramble his hard drives, and a portal would open and flood the basement with lake water. Nothing worthwhile would be retrievable except his wines.

Carrying his go-bag, he moved towards the back door, grabbing a helmet, a leather jacket with spinal protection, some cash, and gloves. Using a different burner phone, he called John Red Crow, a lightly employed neighbor and a good friend. Fortunately, John was both awake and willing to help.

"Can you swing by on the bike?" Jakob asked.

"On my way," replied John.

Within a minute, Jakob heard the dirt bike cough to a start in the distance. John Red Crow pulled onto Jakob's ranch and drove slowly under cover of the trees near the cabin, wearing a helmet and jacket that matched what Jakob had on. He hopped off as Jakob climbed on the Yamaha 450 cross-country bike. Jakob tossed John the keys to his pickup and a roll of fifty-dollar bills.

"It's a pleasure doing business with you, Mr. Red Crow."

Smiling, John flipped and caught the fifties. "The pleasure is all mine."

Jakob gunned the bike, so he emerged from the trees at about the same time Red Crow would have. Then he turned to the north and rode towards Rt. 89. Jakob knew Red Crow would wait ten minutes before he started the truck and began to drive around the 2,300-square-mile reservation for the next ten hours. That should throw off any drone surveillance.

Crossing into Canada went well, and Jakob pulled into Cardston Airport in Alberta. He weaved the bike around the buildings until he found one that advertised charters and parked it under an overhang.

He unzipped then rezipped his jacket. It may have been psychological, but he felt colder in Canada.

According to a sign on the building, the office wouldn't open for almost another hour. That was fine with Jakob because he had things to do. The night before, Jakob had gone back to the basement with heavy scissors and cut the three remaining burner phones out of their overprotective plastic. He took one from his leather jacket and repeated the download and installation process to secure it. Activating the VPN and connecting through a German server, he used Tor to go into the VinsTresBon.com web page. There was one email.

He stared at the blinking icon on the phone.

*I can't figure out why someone is trying to grab me on the one hand while sending me cryptic but cutesy emails on the other. I've already figured out that whoever they are, they aren't trying to kill me. They could have bombed my location, sniped me, or had me poisoned. But the emails just make little sense.*

Before he got distracted by whatever the message was, Jakob downloaded and opened the drone app on his phone to see if anything had happened at his log cabin. After selecting the drone view above his cabin, he saw three men walking around and three horses tied up nearby. Although the video was glitchy and would occasionally freeze, he could tell by their hand signals they were military or ex-military. One man approached the front door and the other the back. A third moved to the trees. Jakob presumed he would provide overwatch while the other two breached.

A chill went down his spine minutes later as he noticed smoke coming from his log cabin. Jakob closed the app as the video showed the first licks of flame enveloping the structure.

*They're burning down my cabin! I helped build that. I need to counter this crap now.*

A honking horn startled him, and he saw a young man climbing out of a Kia Sports car.

"Hi," the man yelled as he walked toward Jakob, "I'm the pilot. You looking to charter a plane?"

Putting the phone in his pocket, Jakob felt his back muscles relax as he replied, "That I am. How far can you fly me with no notice... like now?"

"I've got a King Air 260 Turboprop that can fly seventeen hundred nautical miles, but I've got to say, it's a pricey flight for just one person."

Jakob did some quick calculations in his head to determine where he could go within 1,700 nautical miles. Usually, it wouldn't be a worry because planes would stop and refuel, but someone was clearly hot on his trail. "That'd be great. I'd like to go to Beverly Hills."

The pilot's eyebrows shot up. "You a producer or something?"

Acting insulted, Jakob said, "What, I'm not good-looking enough to be an actor? Why, I've done Hamlet!"

They both laughed.

"Definitely a producer," the pilot said, smiling. "I know when you want to leave. What's the name for the paperwork?"

Jakob paused a second to mentally verify the passport he was using. "Jakob Fugger, it's an EU passport issued in Portugal. How soon can you gas it up?"

"We can be wheels-up in twenty-five minutes, or sooner if my co-pilot makes good time getting here. Want me to work up a quote?"

"You seem like a fair guy to me. No need for a quote or receipt." Jakob handed him a black Amex card registered to one of his family offices. "I would love to get breakfast. Any suggestions nearby?"

The pilot spun around with his arms out, Sound-of-Music style, and said, "We are literally in the middle of nowhere, but I always keep some sandwiches in the office fridge in case I get a short-notice booking. I can have them on the plane with some Diet Cokes. Will that work?"

"That will be great."

He hurried over to the gas truck and started it up as Jakob pulled the phone out again.

# CHAPTER 18

# LIFE 5.0 - HOLLAND 1625

Jakob's second, third, and fourth lives were much simpler than his first and in them, he focused on aspects of life other than business. His trust in adults was low after watching dozens of people he'd tried to help use his gifts for ridiculous and self-destructive undertakings. However, he appreciated the innocence of children, so he funded several orphanages and schools. He had to structure those gifts with caution. If he gave a large amount to an orphanage, it wouldn't be long before a bishop or cardinal would appropriate it.

Jakob traveled a great deal in Life 2.0 as Jakob Lochzwei, improving and expanding his language skills. He learned Mandarin from a student of the explorer and priest, Gaspar Da Cruz.

He also learned Russian, Hebrew, and passable Yiddish. Jakob also grew to respect poetry and loved the bawdy plays of William Shakespeare. In Life 1.0, he had little time for clever turns of phrase, but he was slowing down.

He could access funds he had isolated in his first life without revealing who he was, so earning a living wasn't a driving concern.

Numbered Swiss accounts wouldn't exist for over 300 years, but he had planned well. His Life 2.0 goal was to help people, and when he focused on individuals, he was moderately successful. If he focused on helping large groups of people, Jakob felt he may as well have just thrown gold coins into the ocean.

His third life, however, proved most difficult. It was becoming clear that he wouldn't be dying of old age. At 99, he looked and felt the same as he had in his thirties. Having watched from a distance as his ex-wife, friends, and nephews died, he grew melancholy. His Augsburg businesses split into several smaller ones and most simply closed up. His nephews had run the business diligently, but their children put little effort into it and focused on spending money instead. A sense of *Weltschmerz* or world-weariness overtook Jakob. He continued to help people with his funds and, though he'd had some success in Life 2.0, in 3.0 he met with sparse success.

It seemed people had an infinite ability to screw up their own lives. The French would eventually coin the phrase that captured his feeling, *nostalgie de la boue*, or nostalgia for the mud. It meant that even the most beautiful swan, if born in a mud puddle but moved to a beautiful lake, would self-sabotage until it was back at the mud puddle.

Near the end of Life 3.0, he was living in a small Alsatian village, Riquewihr, where he started a journal to process his thoughts. When he realized how dangerous it would be if found, he burned it. Soon after, Jakob had a life-changing experience.

The year before, he'd confronted and embarrassed the town priest, a man named Franklin. Franklin was, as many were in the sixteenth century, in his position because his family purchased it. His knowledge of and interest in theology was scant, whereas his lust for women was robust. He was flagrantly indiscreet. Jakob confronted him when he cast aside a girl he'd impregnated and started rumors labeling her a prostitute. This drove her from the town and, more than likely, into a life of prostitution.

When confronted, Franklin, far from being contrite, became enraged. He plotted against Jakob and used Jakob's unchanging looks against him. He whipped the town into a fury by claiming the only way someone wouldn't age was through the work of the devil. Jakob ignored it as the idiotic ramblings of a bully, and he was so tired of living with fools, he felt indifferent to the consequences. He was wrong.

One sunset, Franklin appeared at Jakob's house with a mob of townspeople, some actually carrying pitchforks. Franklin called him out, and Jakob plodded to his door, where two men standing on either side grabbed him. They pulled him out and cast him onto the ground. As Jakob rolled over, Franklin seized the moment and threw the first stone, hitting Jakob in the crotch, yelling "Stone the Devil!"

They pelted Jakob with rocks. After three more close-proximity shots to his groin, and several larger rocks hitting his head, he passed out. He awoke before dawn, in more pain than he had ever known. His left arm was useless and dried blood covered his face and clothing. Fortunately, though covered in blood, his head was merely scratched, no teeth broken, and his feet were sore, not mangled. Unsure about his groin, he chose not to investigate until he felt safe. He used his right hand to free himself from the mound of rocks that covered him.

He was in horrible agony, but he was alive. He discovered he wanted to be alive! Through cracked and swollen lips, he slurred aloud to the pile of stones that formerly covered him, "If I live for centuries, it is God's will. But I must avoid further damaging my body if it is going to last me." Although there were hospitals, medicine was rudimentary. Jakob knew too many people that had died from bloodletting to not treat himself. He knew where he could find wintergreen leaves, and drinking tea made from the leaves relieved much of the pain while his body healed.

From that point on, Jakob became security conscious. He was careful not to put himself in physical danger, for the thought of living in pain for hundreds of years had no appeal. He hired large and intimidating servants to act as his security, and they received a bonus every three months if he stayed safe.

It took years, but the Church transferred Franklin to Barcelona as a bishop, a position he hadn't even paid for. Franklin was ecstatic and preached of his promotion as proof of God's justice. He was correct about the justice part. Oddly, he never figured out why the Spanish Inquisition had such detailed records of his indiscretions a year later when they arrested him. The Spanish Inquisition did not deal with rapists gently.

After having survived a stoning in Life 3.0, Jakob reaffirmed his desire to live, and in Life 4.0, he redeemed his love of people. He'd lived over 150 years and had learned how to talk to people, especially women, with skill, if not ease. Inside, he still felt uncomfortable, but he'd trained himself to hide it. He could now look people in their eyes and at least appear to listen patiently while they spoke. He was no longer shy or tongue-tied and had expanded his education to where he could talk about subjects other than commerce.

Much to his surprise, he found that farming was quite pleasant when one's skill as a farmer didn't determine whether he would eat or starve. On warm, dry days, he enjoyed working with his hands and the earth. Perhaps his parents had been onto something, raising them on a farm before moving them to the city. Before his fourth "death," he set the stage for Life 5.0 based in the Netherlands, and he purchased several low-country properties to further his farming adventures.

Living in Amsterdam proved very pleasant, despite the ongoing war between the Dutch and Spain. Another deadly war caused by religious conflicts, for which he carried massive guilt.

Jakob owned several small farms outside the city and enjoyed going out and working the land with his farm managers. He sold his three tulip farms in 1635. He'd agreed only to sell them for an outrageous fortune. Jakob named a price five times what he felt they were worth, but the buyers paid because he grew exquisite, exotic blends of tulips. He felt the deal was too good to be true until he counted the proceeds himself. Twice.

While he made out well on the sale, he mentally kicked himself as already ridiculous prices for tulips went higher and higher for the next two years. To provide a sense of scale for Holland's tulip fever, at its peak, a single tulip bulb could sell for the price of a house. Jakob had sold three 300-acre farms that specialized in growing tulips with inventories of hundreds of thousands of tulip bulbs each. It was a time of madness and rampant speculation. It turned out it was also a good time to hold cash.

The tulip bubble burst two years after he sold, and prices crashed back to reality, and Jakob realized how lucky he'd been to sell when he did. He always imagined someone had finally said, "But they're just flowers!" People were crazy, but he was becoming more tolerant of them the longer he lived.

He was living in Amsterdam, and as far as anyone knew, he was a merchant like so many others in that city, living a comfortable but not ostentatious life. He knew the city well, having been there dozens of times in the last 150 years, starting back when it had been called Amstelldamme.

He owned a house on one of the quieter canals, near a bakery that made bread daily and filled his office with amazing smells. He and his neighbors grew flowers in boxes outside their windows, which reminded him of Augsburg where he grew up. He had investments in several businesses that had grown over time, and he'd invested in several galley ships that sank and were complete write-offs. He benefited from the luxury of time, so when a business didn't go as expected, which was a regular occurrence, he could adjust until it finally succeeded.

He still had almost all the funds he'd set aside from his previous lives and the compound gains that resulted. He left them alone except for one day per year when he would review his investments and either sell or buy something else. His decisions were implemented by bankers he trusted, but still audited. Though he felt he was under-managing the assets, the amounts compounded year after year. He was always careful to change the ownership to his name in the next life before he "died."

Though he knew Amsterdam well, it didn't prevent Jakob from getting lost. The streets of Amsterdam's northern city center are laid out in half circles like an open Asian fan. The cross streets formed arcs that started and ended at the large commercial canal splitting the city. As a result, walking on roads that felt straight but curved confounded him at least once a week.

# CHAPTER 19

# LIFE 18.0 -
# LA 2021

The charter turboprop proved comfortable and fast. However, the sandwiches were horrid. Jakob ate them, nevertheless. *Who puts ketchup on a ham sandwich?*

Jakob asked the pilot to call the Santa Monica Municipal Airport and arrange for a car service to pick him up. Flying private came with some fantastic perks. The pilot was more than happy to help and called ahead as the co-pilot watched the autopilot. Despite Jakob's denials, the pilot seemed convinced that Jakob would meet with some A-List stars. Jakob heard him tell the co-pilot, "Beverly Hills is virtually Hollywood. Why else would anyone fly from Nowhere, Alberta, on a private plane?"

As he climbed into the car after exiting the plane, Jakob popped his head over the roof and yelled over the sound of a plane taking off in the distance, "I'll tell Bobby De Niro you said hi." Jakob smiled as he read the pilot's lips, "I knew it!"

It was another beautiful day in California, and a slight breeze moderated the warm 78-degree air. In the car, Jakob gave the driver an address four blocks over and two blocks down from his beachside house near the Venice Fishing Pier. Then he turned to his burner phone and activated the security software before he logged into his email. There was an email from Hartmann. It took him fifteen minutes to decode it without his computer. Thankfully, it was short.

## Meta and header info suggest the wine email is from Augsburg, Germany.

Jakob then logged into the VinsTresBon.com wine website and opened the message. It was extraordinary.

## AEIOU suggested ICU;

In the sedan's back seat, Jakob felt like he was falling, had to go to the bathroom, and was about to throw up all simultaneously. He felt happy, scared, and disconcertingly aroused. The car ride suddenly felt like a dream. He knew these were signs of going into shock.

*I've given no one enough information to put that phrase together, not even my brothers. I searched for the winking girl for decades with no luck. Someone must be screwing with me, but how could anyone know that?*

Jakob knew what the words meant, but he struggled with their implications. AEIOU was the Motto of the Holy Roman Emperor Frederick II. It stood for *Alles Erdisch ist Osterreich Untertan*, All Earth is Under Austria.

*This message is, or is pretending to be, from the beautiful winking girl dressed in white, that Frederick II called over to "see" me five centuries ago.*

Jakob was struck mute, and she winked at him.

*I have loved her for more than five hundred years. Could this be her? How the hell is she still alive? If it really is her looking for me, why the global search? Why the mercenaries?*

Jakob knew he couldn't let the possibility she was alive ruin his decision-making. So, after a pause where he considered what to say over and over, he wrote back.

**I have been looking for you. How old are you now?**

He opened the back of the phone, and sliding down the car's window, he let the sim card slip from his fingers into the breeze. He slid the battery into his go-bag and slipped the useless phone into the crease of the seats.

*All the rules of dealing with women forbid asking her age, but I can't risk being thrown off by someone throwing around English vowels.*

Jakob entered his house before he realized he'd walked six blocks in a daze and used the biometric scanner without even thinking about it. He moved to the kitchen, which smelled of bleach, and opened a bottle of chilled water from the refrigerator. The cold water pulled him back to the present. He marveled at refrigerators, freezers, and air conditioners—all absolute marvels.

"Okay," he said aloud, trying to talk rationally to the bottle of water. "I'll write it out."

He opened kitchen drawers until he found a pad of paper and a pen and wrote out every question that flowed into his mind, with no evaluation of importance or relevance.

*Can it be the girl who winked?*

*Can it be someone else?*

*If it's the girl who winked, why is she hunting for me so aggressively?*

*Can two people be looking for me at the same time?*

*Have I been followed to LA?*

*Should I rent a car?*

*Should I buy a gun?*

*What can I get for dinner?*

*How quickly can I get to Augsburg?*

*Is Augsburg a trap?*

*How long has the bottled water been in the fridge?*

*Should I order some more wine?*

*How are Hartmann's and Bernthaler's investigations working out?*

The list went on until he filled up two pages, and then Jakob went back and crossed out questions that weren't important. He didn't need to decide about wine or dinner now. He didn't want a gun. Next, he prioritized. Jakob's home office in Venice Beach was like his offices elsewhere, so he got right to work.

First, he called Hartmann, who answered on the first ring, "Hi, sir."

"Hello," Jakob responded. "Any luck on any of the projects?"

"Yes. Mr. B and I," Hartmann began, referring to Bernthaler who handled Jakob's European security, "we found they delivered the wine to a house on Maximilianstraße in Augsburg to a Fraulein K. Weber." He pronounced it as the German name, "Vee-bur. "

Hartmann continued, "We only have the first initial. But we know she lives alone. She paid cash on delivery for the wine, and I'm sure you calculated this already, but it was a lot of cash. Our friends dug deeper and discovered that she had withdrawn the cash from an account at the *Fürst Fugger Privatbank Aktiengesellschaft...*"

Jakob covered his gasp by pretending to cough, then said, "Sorry, please continue." *Fürst Fugger Privatbank Aktiengesellschaft* translated to Prince Fugger Private Bank Stock Corporation. Jakob had almost forgotten that at one point, he'd been elected the Prince-Bishop of Constance.

Hartmann picked up where he'd left off, "I thought that was ironic too. I wonder if you have distant relatives in Augsburg."

Jakob stayed silent.

"Anyway, the account is owned by a shell company. Fraulein Weber has no known associates. Her employment status and sources of her income are unknown. We had no hits on the FBI, CIA, BND, and Interpol databases, at least from the inquiries our friends could make without risking that they get flagged.

"There are over six thousand K. Webers in Germany and Austria. An American church owns the house and has owned it for twenty-two years. A shell company appears to control the church, and the church purchased it from a blind trust twenty-two years ago. It is not clear where Fraulein Weber was before Augsburg. It is as if she just appeared there eight months ago. However, she has no known connection to Russia or the former Soviet countries."

"Very good," Jakob said, overwhelmed by the flood of information, given his focus on K. Weber and the surprise of her banking at a Fugger bank. He covered by asking, "Speaking of Russians, any more on the Russian theory? "

"We scanned the dark web, and there may be something there. From cross-referencing the dark web with some of our private databases, we detected a recent increase in UHNWIs, sorry, I mean Ultra High Net Worth Individuals, looking to buy new identities and disappear themselves."

Jakob interjected, smiling, "I know what UHNWIs are. Thank you."

Hartmann laughed at that. "Yes, I suspect you do. As I was saying, the prices being discussed by these UHNWIs are at the top end.

Also, demand for live pandas is trending up, but that's it from the dark web as far as we could access.

"However, my cousin, who works as a bank regulator in Geneva, mentioned there has been a statistically significant influx of what he called 'ultra large' cash inflows into numbered accounts recently. We could determine that something similar is happening in Panama, and as odd as it sounds, South Dakota. We're looking into other locales with strong banking secrecy."

"Now that is interesting," responded Jakob. South Dakota made sense to Jakob. In the 1980s, the state made dynastic trusts legal, cut regulations, and fortified banking secrecy to bring in estate management businesses. Obviously, it was working.

Hartmann continued, "Yes, it is. It implies that there may be more UHNWIs getting squeezed. After an in-depth analysis, we determined the panda demand is unrelated, but the people looking to disappear themselves are worrying."

"Thorough analyses like the panda one are why you make the big bucks," Jakob said, smiling.

Totally deadpan, Hartmann moved on. "Do you want me to assemble a protective detail?"

Jakob thought for a moment. "I'd like you to start the process, based in Munich, at least a dozen men to be ready in two or three days."

Jakob updated Hartmann about what happened on the Blackfeet reservation. Hartmann absorbed the implications with a simple, "Well, shit."

"I have a thought, and it involves the Romanians," Jakob told him. "Please reach out to the team of hackers we've used there before and find out their availability to help. "

Being willing to spend a lot of money doesn't guarantee you can get the very best hackers on-demand. Being the best for hire also meant they were almost always in high demand, and Jakob absolutely wanted the best for what he was considering.

Hartmann agreed, then warned, "Be very cautious."

Jakob took Hartmann's advice. If whoever was tracking him had the resources he suspected they did, it wouldn't be long until they realized he flew to LA. The Beverly Hills breadcrumbs he left with the pilot would throw them off, but only for a short time.

Jakob knew he had to leave the US soon, and yet he didn't want to disregard his regular work. One lesson learned after hundreds of years is that focusing exclusively on a current crisis at the expense of other priorities rarely paid off. Jakob signed on and checked some timetables before he got down to his everyday work. He checked email and then checked the wine site after launching his VPN, and there was another message.

**J, I hope you like old women. I was born the same year as the powerful Anne of France. Time 4U2CMe.**

There were thousands of Annes in France, but only one had been truly powerful. The daughter of Louis XI, helpfully named "Anne of France," was the Regent of France until her younger brother grew old enough to rule. She would have been born around 1460 or 1461.

*Is it possible? It might be. If I gained unexplained longevity, maybe I wasn't alone. There's no reason that only one person from Augsburg, born in the mid-1400s, could live for centuries. Perhaps their longevity was induced by something in the environment or a virus that, rather than killing us, made us resistant to death. Maybe whatever protected the town during the Black Death is living on in us and protecting us from regular death.*

*Some animals live for hundreds of years, trees for thousands, and some jellyfish are biologically immortal. Maybe it's a trap. But I'm thinking it isn't.*

Jakob knew he must be very careful because he hadn't been this excited in a long time. He knew he was likely to make mistakes feeling like this. So, sitting alone in his office, Jakob asked himself aloud, "How do I get to Augsburg and stay free?"

Then he answered himself aloud, and it sounded to him like it might work.

Jakob refused to allow himself to fine-tune his plan until he had done his regular work. Fine-tuning his plan would be his reward.

For the first sixty years of his life, he wanted only to make as much money as possible without compromising his principles. Now, making money was more of a reflex than a driving ambition. Ironically, Jakob found he spent much more time structuring legal arrangements to obscure his compounding wealth than he spent trying to earn more.

He thought back to the conversation he'd had with the Montana security guard, Thomas Brown Claw, as they worked together to get gambling legalized on the reservation. One night, they were talking about meetings in Manhattan, which Thomas kept referring to as "the $24 island." He was referring to the amount for which the Lenape Indians sold Manhattan to the Dutch in the early seventeenth century.

"The white man, once again, totally screwed the Indians on that one," said Brown Claw.

"I agree white men have screwed Native Americans on a lot of things, but let's look a bit more closely at that deal," responded Jakob.

Having worked with Jakob before, Thomas Brown Claw closed his eyes and dropped his chin to his chest, knowing he was about to get another financial lecture. Which, of course, he was.

"In 1626, a Dutchman, Peter Minuit, paid sixty guilders to buy Manhattan Island from the Lenape Indians. Let's just stipulate those sixty guilders were worth twenty-four dollars. 1626 was a long time ago. If the Lenape had invested those twenty-four dollars in something that returned about nine percent a year, which is less than the average return of the US stock market since its inception, what do you think it would be worth today?"

"If I weren't talking to you, I would guess maybe a hundred and fifty thousand bucks. But you wouldn't be asking if it weren't a shit-ton of money, so I'm going to guess one billion with a 'B,' dollars," responded Brown Claw.

"Impressive. That's more than I thought you would guess," admitted Jakob, giving Thomas an approving nod, "but the real answer is around $650 trillion, with a 'T.' That's six hundred fifty thousand billion. The land value of Manhattan today is a trifling $2 trillion."

"You're shitting me!" said Brown Claw, astounded, and wide awake. "Six hundred fifty trillion, with a motherfucking 'T'?"

"I shit you not," said Jakob, smiling. He was prouder of the fact he knew the right response to the vernacular "you're shitting me" than of making his point about the massive effect time has on compounding returns.

"We totally screwed the white man on that deal!" Brown Claw smiled.

125

Jakob just smiled back. In 1625, when he first "died," Jakob had set aside a "shit-ton" more than sixty guilders.

In today's world, he couldn't simply keep a checking account with trillions of dollars in it and keep it secret. Jakob knew that visible and traceable assets would make it difficult to keep his life private, particularly as reporting requirements intensified worldwide and private accounts were less private with each passing year.

Jakob, therefore, had to change the way his assets were compounding and how some were being held. So, for the last two decades, he had been burying treasure.

The copper and silver mines he owned in Hungary in Life 1.0 had run dry long ago. Twenty years ago, Jakob repurchased three of the defunct mines through layers of shell companies. He immediately hired engineering teams to stabilize and expand the shafts, and he uncreatively named them the Red Mine, the Blue Mine, and the Yellow Mine.

Then he created a cover story. After fortifying the fencing around the mines, he created dozens of concrete, water, and lead fail-safes within the mines themselves, and then they were ready. He couldn't risk his buried treasure being discovered, so he applied to the Hungarian Atomic Energy Authority for permits to store radioactive waste in the mines.

Fortunately, the environmental review, which he feared could derail his plan, split 50/50 among the factions of the European Greens. Half of the Green organizations that submitted comments claimed he was a devil dealing with the world's most toxic pollution and Hungary should deny his permits. The other half argued he was putting radioactive waste deep underground, where most of it came from. It was the least awful way to store the world's most toxic pollution, and Hungary should approve his permits.

Thus, within a few years, triple-sealed barrel-shaped dry casks made of concrete and steel arrived at the mine, and they were color-coded. Red barrels were lowered into the Red Mine, and the same color matching went for the Blue and Yellow barrels. All the barrels were heavy. By design, the dry cask barrels were so tight that almost no radiation leaked out.

In the Yellow Mine, the Geiger counters didn't detect any radiation. Only two people, Jakob and the Yellow Mine manager, knew that if someone cracked the barrels open, no radiation would leak because they didn't contain spent radioactive fuel. They contained his gold.

Buying and securing the mines turned out to be the easiest part of his plan. The reason it took an additional eighteen years was that the market for gold was finicky. Jakob had to cash out his positions and buy gold slowly in a manner that wouldn't spike the price up too far. It took almost exactly eighteen years to bury 10% of Jakob's treasure in the form of gold. As he developed his plan, he assumed that gold would be stable, and, with the elimination of the gold standard in the US, it would not increase much in value. Instead, it would just hold its value for a long time. Jakob's assumption was wrong, and the price of gold increased by over 9% per year over the previous twenty years.

In his underground beach office, Jakob checked on the price of gold and his other investments. There did not appear to be any new fires to put out. Two hours later, he finished with his regular work, and allowed himself to work on his reward: planning his trip to Augsburg.

Jakob's fingers flew over the keyboard, checking schedules, routes, rates, satellite pictures, maps, and weather. He opened a spreadsheet and laid it all out, then went back and verified each of his assumptions.

*My plan should work!*

Chapter 20 - Life 5.0 Dutch East India Company - 1629

Draining loneliness and the beauty of Dutch women led Jakob to break his vow never to marry again. While different from Italian women, Dutch women were striking. The Dutch were straightforward, which he appreciated, because although he'd improved at reading facial expressions, nonverbal cues and understanding sarcasm, it did not come naturally to him. Sporadically, the Dutch bluntness stung, such as when a woman informed him he could be attractive if he just had different lips, perhaps a different nose, and, well, if his eyes weren't quite the way they were. Ironically, she liked Jakob and wasn't trying to be insulting. She was just being Dutch.

He found a woman who liked him with his face arranged the way it was, and she was lovely. Edda was smart, funny, and practical. He liked her very much, even though he did not get the same intensity of feeling he'd felt with the winking girl 170 years before.

He thought back to that moment when she'd winked at him thousands of times, and for a while, in Life 2.0, he'd convinced himself he suffered from what the doctors then called "bad humors" and they were what made him feel dizzy, happy, aroused, and drawn to her. But the longer he lived, the less he believed it was bad humors.

Edda, though not as magnetic as the winking girl, was almost always in a good mood and great fun to be around. Her laugh was contagious, and her eyes sparkled as if she were always planning some joke or trick. She almost always was. Filled with practical knowledge, she had no interest in finance.

She loved Jakob. She loved life. And she loved raising children. They had more than enough to live comfortably, and that was fine with her. Any further discussion of his day or dealings, particularly involving commerce, resulted in her eyes glazing over. If Jakob droned on too long and missed the nonverbal cues that she wasn't following him, he risked getting hit with whatever she was holding. Edda had impressive aim when throwing kitchen implements.

They were very compatible and had two boys soon after they married. When his sons were about 10, Jakob tried to teach them about investments. Edda would roll her eyes and try not to smile as they stood in front of Jakob, attempting to recite back to him the difference between the interest and the principal. He loved learning from his mother about business, and he struggled to believe that his sons didn't enjoy it as well.

Jake, his elder son, grew to have a basic understanding of investing, but he had little interest. Though an intelligent young man, he was uncommonly handsome, and compound returns could not compete with the allure of the girls who swarmed around him like moths around a flame.

Daan, Jakob's younger son, focused on a single aspect of wealth: spending money. He was interested in it and growing up in a well-off family affected him in ways Jakob never expected. Daan did as little work as possible. He earned low grades in his classes, and Jakob discovered he was imperious to others. Daan considered himself superior to others only because his family had money. Lacking his mother's and brother's charm, Daan had few friends.

Of course, he did not know his father's true wealth, but he felt far superior to his peers and treated them as if they were his servants. Jakob spoke to him several times with increasing intensity and anger about acting like an ass, and Daan would appear contrite.

A few weeks later, however, Daan would be back at it, and Jakob would discover that he had done almost none of his schoolwork. Daan agreed with all of Jakob's and Edda's arguments, but he simply would not do what he agreed to do.

After herculean parental effort compelled him to finish something, once done, he would act as if he had done it with no prompting. He went so far as to use it as an example of something he'd done with no support and demand his parents get off his back. It reached a point that Jakob wanted to evict Daan from their home, but he was still a boy, and Edda hoped he would grow out of it.

One day, Jakob received an official notice saying that one of his smaller investments in a spice trading company was now merged with others through a government decree. The combined entities formed the Vereenigde Oostindische Compagnie, or VOC, better known as the Dutch East India Company. While Jakob disliked the government's compelling businesses to do anything, he did not sell his interests immediately because this combination had created a new business structure. A structure which intrigued him.

Rather than finance a single ship for a single voyage and then collapse the company when it returned or sank, the VOC stayed active and funded multiple ships multiple times. It traded textiles, spice, and silk and was an altogether new form of organization called a "corporation." It issued both shares and bonds to the public, and ownership of the shares provided protections if the company went out of business.

Up to that point, Jakob's investments in the spice trading company came with risk. If something went tragically wrong with the venture, as an owner, Jakob was liable for damages above and beyond his original investment. The old venture could have cost him everything held in his name, including his properties and assets.

Jakob tried to explain this to Edda in her new kitchen. They had moved to a more prosperous area on a beautiful canal that had arched bridges on either side of the house. The width of houses in Amsterdam determined the tax due, so most were tall and narrow. Jakob had purchased two narrow houses and had them combined into a wider home for his family. It was an ostentatious move for him, but he disliked narrow houses. The new kitchen was enormous, with windows that flooded it with light, and as Edda was making bread one day, Jakob struggled to convey his infatuation with the corporation.

He received an impressive eye roll of incomprehension from his first attempt, so he tried a different tactic. "Imagine the old way of structuring a business was like heating our home with a fire pit in the middle of the floor."

"Why would we have a fire pit in the middle of the house?" She gave him a look she normally reserved for when he made a social blunder.

He continued, "This is hypothetical. Anyway, everything is fine if the fire is controlled, but if the fire gets out of control, our house will burn, and maybe the family with it."

"I don't know what a hypothetical is, but I will assume you're making up a false situation as an allegory for what you are trying to convey."

Jakob just smiled as she continued, kneading bread as she spoke, "So I assume this corporation is different from you burning down our house and us all dying?"

"Yes!" Jakob responded, more excitedly than the situation justified. "In this new, corporate way of doing things, the fire stays in a structure outside the house, so only the heat comes into the house, not the flames. If the fire gets out of control, the other structure burns, but our house and family will be safe."

"Oh, certainly," she said, "why would you ever go with the old way of doing things and risk burning everything?"

"Exactly! If you had the choice, you wouldn't." He kissed her cheek and tasted the salty flour that covered it, as she mumbled, "You'll never design a house we'll live in..."

Failing to read the room, Jakob continued, "Bonds issued by the company are interesting in their own way. With the bonds, if the venture fails, the bond owners can take over the equity ownership and sell assets to get their money back. If it does well, the bondholders will receive their full payments but not get any further payments."

Edda lifted an egg-sized ball of dough in her hand, testing its weight, but he continued, "If I could find a buyer, I could sell my stock and bonds whenever I wanted. I don't need the blessing of the other investors." Jakob's enthusiasm was on full display.

The dough ball hit him in the middle of his forehead, knocking him back into the wall. Edda looked at him for a moment. "You're lucky you are pretty because you make no sense sometimes."

Jakob took that as a victory. Edda thought he was pretty. He smiled as he wiped his forehead and took a bite of the salty, sweet dough.

The VOC was a wonder for its time. And looking back, it seems even more wondrous now because nobody had ever done it before. The company hired managers because they knew how to manage, not because they were relatives. They ran their business like Jakob tried to run his businesses in previous lives.

In the mid-seventeenth century, Dutch ships would be outfitted and sent off with a general set of instructions. There could be three or four exchanges of letters between the captain and the VOC during a typical voyage, or there could just as easily be no communication at all. Letters from the Netherlands had to be carried by other ships going to where the first ship was supposed to be. The target ship may be there, or it may not. The ship with the letter may get there on time, or it may not. Decision-making came down to the captain, and the captains had an economic stake in how their ships performed. Because of that, the VOC prospered.

The VOC became the largest commercial company in the world, and it proved to be a very lucrative investment for Jakob. He invested the profits from his other ventures into the VOC and reached a point where he became one of VOC's largest shareholders, which brought too much attention. He then spread out the investments, so they were made not by him but by various businesses he controlled. Almost painful to him, he also sold some of his shares. Even in the seventeenth century, he did not want publicity.

Jakob's older son, Jake, found and married a girl he loved. After working on his own for several years, Jake came into the family business and enjoyed it. Jakob's younger son, Daan, grew into a man. To Daan's disappointment, he looked more like Jakob than Edda. He aged, but he did not mature.

Daan lost one job after another and racked up debts from wagering. He'd reached a point where he risked being sent to jail when Jakob sat him down and had a mountain of guilders on the table between them that would allow Dann to pay off his debts three times over. Jakob offered him three choices.

First, he could come to work with his brother and Jakob, earning thirty times the guilders in the pile. But he would have to work and pay his debts from his income.

Second, he could take the mound of guilders, but that would be it. If he took the money, Jakob would no longer support him.

Third, he could do neither, pull his life together and get himself out of debt, and at some later time come to work with them or work for an outside firm as a self-made man.

Daan took the guilders.

Of course, he spent the money in months. He came back wanting more, but Jakob would not give in. It hurt him more than he expected, for when he looked at Daan, Jakob saw himself. It hurt Edda even more and strained their marriage when Daan disappeared and didn't speak to his family for years.

Decades later, Jakob discovered Daan had returned to Amsterdam, matured somewhat, and worked as a courier for one of his brother's competitors.

# CHAPTER 21

# LIFE 18.0 - LEAVING LA 2021

Jakob was up before dawn, having barely slept as thoughts of the winking girl cycled through his mind.

*What if she stopped aging at a different age than me? I don't care if she looks older than me, but what if she stopped aging at 16? What if she is married? I have loved her for five hundred years, and she could be married to someone else. What if she doesn't like me once we meet? She could be sick or dying. What if she is bitter? We may be incompatible. What if it isn't everything I've built it up to be?*

*Okay...stop whining.*

*I will check it out cautiously. But I will check it out.*

Jakob entered the tunnel that started under his beach house and walked, his go-bag in hand. Aside from its normal contents, the bag held additional burner phones and three peanut butter and jelly sandwiches. Jakob had learned his lesson from the plane ride from Canada.

The tunnel felt cool and, though he'd built it decades ago, it still smelled like freshly poured concrete. Clean and dry, the tunnel led him beneath the yard of a neighboring house on the street behind his street. At the tunnel's end, he climbed a hard resin ladder, entered a different code into a trapdoor at the top, and emerged into the darkened shed in the backyard of a neighbor who received $650 a month to allow Jakob to store stuff in her shed. He exited and walked through the cool predawn morning to the street where an Uber waited to pick him up.

The Uber took him to a brilliantly lit 24-hour superstore where he bought an inexpensive Chromebook and some Diet Coke. It was no trouble for him to find the taxi waiting for him in the massive, empty parking lot, and the driver took him twenty-five minutes away and stopped under an overpass. Jakob exited, tipped a forgettable amount, and climbed the concrete embankment to the road above where a brightly colored Flexibus loaded customers.

He paid the $19 bus fare to Las Vegas in cash, and once inside, climbed to the top level and sat at the front, above the driver. The Chromebook booted, and soon Jakob connected to the Wi-Fi on the bus. Creating a throwaway Gmail account, he booked a flight to Zurich, with two stops where he wouldn't exit the plane.

If someone chased him across the globe, they would have profiled him. They would know that he avoided flights that had multiple stops. They would also feel confident that he would take a direct flight or a private flight. If it turned out that "JF ICU" was a trap to get him to Augsburg, they would be waiting for him at the private Flughafen Augsburg airport or at Munich's International Airport. Zurich was only a three-hour drive from Augsburg, but there were many better choices if you wanted to get to Augsburg quickly.

The Flexibus was the first bus Jakob had been on in decades. Although it proved comfortable and clean, traveling by bus fell far outside his standard travel protocol.

# CHAPTER 22

# LIFE 10.0 -
# RED SHIELD 1769

Many people live their lives following the path of their parents, their culture, their king's will, or their religion. "Blessed are the meek, for they shall inherit the earth" was perhaps the single most effective ambition-crushing phrase Jakob could think of. Put back in their place early and regularly, most people stayed in their place. They challenged little, learned little, and taught their children to do the same to save them from disappointment.

In 1769, Jakob had been alive for 310 years, and his obfuscated fortune continued growing. Every so often, through the intelligence network Jakob established, he received word of someone both intelligent and a freethinker. Such word reached him in 1769. He was living Life 9.0 as Jakob Altermann, German for "old man," and he heard of a coin trader named Rothschild in Frankfurt on Main who sounded quite sharp. He had just been appointed "Court Jew" to the very wealthy Crown Prince Wilhelm of Hesse, who reported directly to the Holy Roman Emperor. It was a significant position for Rothschild, even with its degrading title.

Jakob was living near Frankfurt on Main and made his way to the Jewish ghetto there, thinking he could meet with the coin trader. The ghetto was overcrowded because Frankfurt law confined all 3,000 Jews in Frankfurt to live in the small two-block ghetto set aside for them. The buildings were designed for 175 families.

Rothschild's shop was at the end of the muddy alley that reeked of the manure of the hundreds of horses that filled it during the days, making and picking up deliveries. The building, like its neighbors, was wood timbered and five stories tall. The front of his shop looked tidy and well-appointed, with brass and glass displays and it smelled of brass polish, which Jakob preferred to the smell of manure that filled the alley.

Jakob had some coins he'd collected over time and presented them to Rothschild for an appraisal. The coins were rare for the eighteenth century and of such high quality that the coin trader closed for the day, and the two men talked.

Rothschild's intense eyes gave him gravitas that belied his young age. He knew a great deal about coins and money. He asked Jakob about the provenance of several of the coins he'd brought. "One rarely sees coins this old with no degradations," he said.

Coins in circulation at the time, particularly old coins, had "bits" snipped out of them by someone who only needed a percentage of the value of a coin. One bit was one-eighth of a coin, and two bits was a quarter. Those coins that didn't have bits removed frequently had their edges shaved by untrustworthy men.

Jakob's coins had neither. Rothschild asked, "How did you come by these?"

Jakob responded, "Herr Rothschild, they have been in my family's possession since just after they were minted. My people came from Augsburg," he explained, "and I wonder how you would value them."

"Please call me Mayer," he insisted. "It will take me some time to come up with a fair price for these, but it will be a pleasure to work with you on it." As he weighed, took notes, and made drawings of the coins, Jakob asked him about himself and his plans. Though outwardly modest, Jakob determined that Rothschild held aspirations far higher than being a Court Jew. Jakob asked innocent-sounding questions to gauge whether he was a man of means, talking of wine, travel, and the court of the emperor. Rothschild knew and cared little for wine or travel, but he proved very astute and well-informed about the court of the emperor and the various princes. He admitted he was too busy to look for a wife, had no friends in Frankfurt, only acquaintances, and rarely saw his family. But he announced proudly, he planned to have a large family one day and bring his sons into the business.

The name Jakob was more commonly associated with Jews than with Gentiles. For hundreds of years, Jakob had been called a Jew, accused of being a Jew, and charged with usury, the Christian crime of lending for interest. While the Church prohibited Christians from lending for interest for centuries, nothing prohibited Jews from lending. They were, however, prohibited from doing many things that Christians took for granted, and so, with most occupations closed off to them, many Jews became moneylenders. Ironically, the followers of Jesus, who was Jewish, hated the Jews. As Jakob also lent money, he suspected borrowers blamed religious differences every time a Jewish moneylender came to collect.

Because of the hate and scorn aimed at him and having been a moneylender, Jakob felt he had developed an appreciation for the challenges facing Jews in Europe. In a previous life, he had taught himself Hebrew, and a smattering of Yiddish, with the help of an attractive Jewish female tutor.

When Rothschild mentioned he was Ashkenazi, Jakob asked him in Hebrew if he knew where in central Europe his family was from, and his heavy eyebrows lifted. Then, in Yiddish, Rothschild responded, "You are Jewish."

"As are you," Jakob replied in Yiddish, not answering.

Jakob must have passed the test because Rothschild gathered up Jakob's coins with a laugh and handed them back. Then, striding into the back room, he dropped some of his own coins into a velvet bag, and he invited Jakob to dine with him. They spent the night eating and drinking at a crowded ratskeller, with Rothschild doing most of the talking.

The coin trader had the voracious appetite of a draft horse, and took massive bites of food, twisting his fork when needed to get them into his mouth. He consumed one and a half roast chickens, while Jakob ate one half of the smaller bird. The carrots were cooked perfectly, and they both had a helping of fried dough, still hot inside. An Alsatian Riesling complemented everything.

Swaying a bit, Jakob assumed from his considerable consumption of wine, Rothschild brought the coins out from his velvet bag and spilled them on the table. They were old coins, obscure to almost anyone unless that person studied coins or had been alive when they were in use. Jakob recognized this as another test, and appreciating the irony, he picked up the most valuable, a gold coin from the early 1620s.

It felt strange to hold a coin he'd held before, a coin minted in his own mint with his name stamped in the gold on its face. "I haven't seen a 1621 Fugger ten ducat in a long time," Jakob said with a smile, being truthful.

Mayer was suddenly sober and very suspicious. "You know much about coins. Why then do you come to me wanting to know the value of your coins?" he demanded.

Jakob calmly replied, "I wanted to meet you, and I want to sell the coins." He sipped his wine and continued, "I would be a fool to walk into an expert's shop and open negotiations by stating, 'I want to sell you these coins.' I wanted you to covet them before we talked about price."

A small smile crossed Rothschild's face as he nodded. "That is a fair strategy. I like you. Join me for lunch tomorrow at my shop. I will have good prices for you."

The next day, Jakob returned to the shop, where Mayer Rothschild had set up a spread in his back room with food enough to serve four people, this time with both chicken and duck. Rothschild's back room was small, with small cubbies climbing the side and back walls with sacks of coins in them. The smell of the cooked duck filled the room, and Jakob's mouth watered.

In the center of the office sat a walnut table Rothschild used as a desk. Jakob's host had opened another wine, a Spätburgunder, the German pinot noir. Mayer had been evaluating Jakob while Jakob was evaluating him.

"This is very nice, Mayer, thank you," Jakob said as the coin trader waved him to a seat. They sat, and lifting glasses, they simultaneously said "L'chaim." To life. Little did Jakob know then that Rothschild's life would be so abbreviated.

Rothschild ate as they talked about coin prices. On about the tenth coin, in midsentence, Rothschild stopped talking, and after several seconds, Jakob looked up. Rothschild's face was bright red, and he was clawing at his cravat, choking. Jakob jumped up and pounded Rothschild's back as his lips went from red to blue, but soon thereafter, Rothschild fell out of his chair, landing dead on the floor.

Jakob jumped up, stunned. The Frankfurt police didn't come into the ghetto, except to harass the Jews. Rothschild had mentioned he hadn't seen his family in years. As Jakob righted the chair and picked up the jacket that had hung over the back, he heard an urgent, almost violent, banging on the front door. Jakob went to answer it, Rothschild's coat in his hands, and a man frantically ran in when the lock turned.

"Herr Rothschild, thank God you're here. I need to sell these immediately! I need the money as soon as possible. My son was arrested."

He dropped five Charles VI French Silver Blanc Guenars on the table. "What can you give me for these?"

"I'm sorry to say that..." Jakob began, ready to explain Rothschild's death, but the man cut Jakob off, gesticulating like a madman.

"Please, it is a matter of life or death," he interrupted. Tears streamed down his flushed face.

Moved by his genuine fear, Jakob named a fair price, and the man thanked him as Jakob paid him from the money in his purse.

Grabbing Jakob's hand and shaking it, he said, "Mayer Rothschild, you are truly a great man," and dashed from the shop.

Jakob locked the door after he left, sat back down at the table in the back room and downed his wine as a thought percolated in his mind. Then, talking to the dead body of Mayer Rothschild, he said aloud, "Well, this could be interesting," as he slid his arm into Rothschild's coat. Thus began Jakob's rebirth in Life 10.0 as Mayer Amschel Rothschild.

# CHAPTER 23

# LIFE 18.0 - ZURICH 2021

Getting off the bus from Los Angeles, it amazed Jakob that the Las Vegas airport had slot machines throughout, and all of them were in use.

*Man will not pass up an opportunity to make statistically terrible decisions. The house always wins and never more so than with slot machines where the odds of winning are 1 in 50 million.*

Jakob learned that fact while helping to establish tribal gambling with the Blackfeet Nation. Despite its attempt to take the last few dollars from its visitors, the Vegas airport proved clean, air-conditioned, and efficient, and he arrived at the airport security check-in within twenty minutes of being dropped off.

His unique hat altered the appearance of his face. He kept it powered on until ten seconds before his passport verification. Jakob then looked down and away from the cameras during those seconds, hoping his evasive tactics would be mistaken for awkward shyness. The moment he passed through passport control, using his Dominica passport, he turned the hat back on.

The flight was long, and the young but sturdy woman in front of Jakob immediately inclined her seat after takeoff and began snoring.

*I'm embarrassed by how much I dislike flying coach.*

Though Jakob had flown in early planes made of cloth, rope, and pine where the engine smoke blew forcefully into his face, this flight was among the most uncomfortable he'd ever taken. Jakob felt little consolation that the woman snoring in front of him slept through both layovers and awoke refreshed as they approached Zurich. Before landing, Jakob went to the toilet and put the sparkle cream on his face. Fortunately, it didn't sparkle unless a bright light shined on it.

*They must design it to only refract light in a camera.*

He felt ridiculous, but it was a cost of staying free. Although he felt the probability of mercenaries waiting at Zurich airport was low, he didn't want to take chances. As he moved with the crowd towards baggage claim, he noticed the number of Flughafenpolizei, airport police, started to grow exponentially. He reached into his go-bag and removed the electronic blocker that Hartmann had given him and a burner phone. He didn't have time to set up the burner securely, so he called Bernthaler and told him to be at passenger drop-off, not pick-up, for Air France in five minutes then hung up, broke the phone, and dropped the Sim card.

The Flughafenpolizei presence was now noticeably large, and a spherical man, huffing from the exertion of walking, turned and gave Jakob a quick look, brows arched, while silently mouthing, "What the heck?"

Jakob leaned over and whispered, "You think there are enough police?"

"Fucking Nazis," said his walking partner, who then bumped Jakob with his canvas carry-on, and shuffled himself into the men's room, looking like he might pass out. The canvas bag was embroidered with the initials "ASS," which Jakob found very fitting.

The security detail formed into a gauntlet, which allowed them to check out everyone leaving the customs area. About thirty seconds before Jakob reached the gauntlet, the police who'd formed the gauntlet raced *en masse* to the men's room. Jakob moved to the stairs, climbed to the passenger drop-off floor, and once outside, spotted Bernthaler sitting behind the wheel of an Iveco work truck with a red and gold Toblerone logo on the side.

Jakob looked at him as the passenger door opened. As Jakob climbed in, Bernthaler smiled. "*Hallo*, this seemed like one of the least likely executive transport vehicles for a jet-setting world traveler. How was the trip?"

Jakob had to agree and said, "This works for me, and it has much more legroom than my plane seat. Not very restful, and they have flagged my passports. I dropped an electronic scrambler in the carry-on of a rather small-minded American, and he drew the armed attention of the authorities before they could focus their attention on me. We should leave now."

The truck pulled away, and Bernthaler handed Jakob a Toblerone hat and heavy black glasses with clear lenses.

Putting on the hat and glasses, Jakob said, "Thank you. Any updates?"

As they drove quickly through the immaculate streets of Zurich, Bernthaler summarized. "Fraulein Weber leaves her house most days at noon and goes to the Viktualien Feinkost grocery, and then gets coffee at Il Gabbiano on Maximilianstraße. She then goes back home.

"Hartmann asked that I tell you that the Romanians will be available in four days and that he thinks there is very likely a Slavic connection. You aren't the only person targeted. Several people on the Forbes list have also fallen off the grid." He handed Jakob a plastic bag. In it were more burner phones, thankfully already unpackaged.

"All of that is excellent information, thank you."

Bernthaler drove in silence after that, and Jakob appreciated it as he worked through the implications of what Bernthaler told him.

*The winking girl, if that is who she is, is not hiding. She is taking daily walks and following the same routine. If it is the Russians, and other UHNWIs are slipping off the grid, this is economically based and has nothing to do with longevity, thank God! Perhaps the Russian president has decided to go global with his money grab. It worked splendidly for him with his oligarchs, so why not? If the Romanians will be available in four days, that gives me only four days to get a month's worth of work done.*

The city of Ramnicu Valcea in Romania is famous for both the best cyber security experts and the best hackers. As a result, it has earned the nickname "Hackerville." The group Jakob wanted was from Ramnicu Valcea, but they now worked out of Moldova because working in Hackerville proved too cliche.

Jakob used a burner to check the wine site. There were no new messages. Her last message asked Jakob to see her.

*And see her, I will.*

They crossed into Germany with no problems. The European Union had made travel in Europe almost frictionless. The trip from Zurich took about three hours, and Jakob woke up on the approach to Augsburg. He hadn't realized he'd fallen asleep, but he awoke feeling refreshed, even as darkness settled over the town.

"Please drop me off outside the city gates," he said, giving Bernthaler the GPS coordinates.

They soon arrived at the land he grew up farming until he was 10 years old. "I know of some excellent hotels in Augsburg," offered Bernthaler when he saw the ancient farmhouse. "I could take you there."

Chuckling, Jakob responded, "No, thank you. This will be fine."

The farmhouse Bernthaler reacted to was a reconstructed version of the one Jakob had grown up in. He'd bought the land hundreds of years ago, and paid artisans to recreate the farmhouse from his memory, albeit more sturdily. More recently, he'd added a particular basement under the farmhouse. As Jakob stepped down from the cab of the truck, a warm melancholy overcame him as it did every time he visited. He let the overripe smell of the ground, the pollen in the air, and the faint bitter smell of old thatching fill his lungs. The night was cool, and he felt the chill on his wrists and neck.

"*Danke*," Jakob thanked Bernthaler as he handed him back the hat and glasses. "I will be in touch, but please have men near the grocery, ready to go tomorrow before noon."

Bernthaler looked at him as if to verify if Jakob was serious about the timeline, and Jakob just smiled and gave him a small nod.

*It's time.*

As Jakob walked through the farmhouse, he felt ambivalent. Part of him wanted to walk the worn floor planks and reminisce about his childhood, but the practical part of him wanted to get to the basement and start working. His cramped timeline made the decision easy, so he coded into the basement and turned on the computers. Using every bit of cryptology tradecraft he had, Jakob wrote a letter to the head of the Romanian team. He expected that the Romanian would trace the email to Augsburg, but Jakob took the precautions out of respect.

> Hello, my friend. I have a very challenging, risky, and rewarding project. Since we last worked together, I believe you married a Ukrainian girl. Congratulations, by the way. I mention that because I'm sure you remember the damage that NotPetya did to the Ukrainians. Almost as much damage as was done to the Crimea. I would like to create an updated, more surgically controlled, version of NotPetya to threaten the terrible man or group behind all of this, as well as FancyBear, which I suspect is involved in this mess and the NotPetya one.

He pressed send. NotPetya, or GoldenEye in English, was a program developed by FancyBear, the notorious Russian government's in-house group of hackers. NotPetya initially attacked accounting software in Ukraine. Every time an accountant would connect to a client's system, the virus would infect that system and then spread while staying dormant.

However, one day the virus came alive and encrypted all the accounting systems and banking systems it touched. It shut down businesses. It wiped people out. Ukrainians lost billions of *hryvnia*, their currency. NotPetya also disabled radiation monitoring systems at Chernobyl. The team of Romanian hackers Jakob had just emailed was key in stopping NotPetya's damage.

Someone wanted to capture him. Someone that knew about a portion of his wealth and had determined they deserved some of it. They didn't know the true extent of his wealth, and he could use that to his advantage.

Jakob knew he could not turn to the police or the State Department. As a rich, old white guy, his was not a sympathetic story, and he had no interest in exposing his life to the government.

He had been successful in the past by being a clever capitalist. He believed unflinchingly that a lightly regulated free market was a great thing and that credit and lending were the lubrication of the economic machine. A robust economy helped everyone involved.

History supported his position. Pure socialism or communism failed at everything except ensuring everyone was equally poor and miserable, except those that ran the countries. Even recently, the richest truly socialist country was Cuba, where the average wage was under $400 per year. Even if both parents worked, the average Cuban family of four was financially seventy-five times worse off than a poor American one.

He felt that any thinking adult in the twenty-first century knew this implicitly, but some felt it was fashionable to denigrate the system that provided them with their lifestyles. Every so often, he found himself talking with someone who enjoyed the benefits of capitalism but presented themselves as anti-bank, anti-money, anti-capitalism, and very anti-rich-old-guys.

That happened recently at a rare bookstore in Manhattan where the manager was grumbling about the horrors of capitalism as she wrapped his $680 book purchase. Not surprisingly, bankers bore the brunt of her anger. As she poked a manicured finger at a bank notice informing her that she'd overdrawn her business checking account, she said, "I'd be fine if there were no banks, and all bankers had to work as rice farmers."

Jakob had purchased tens of thousands of dollars of her books and generally kept a low profile, so it surprised her when he spoke up. "Imagine where you would live and what you would drive if there was no credit, and you had to pay cash for your co-op and your car. Imagine what you would earn if your shop could have no credit, and you couldn't take credit cards. Imagine the limited services the government would provide if it couldn't borrow. How many businesses like yours would never open if every vendor had to be paid in cash? A cash-only, no-borrowing economy, or worse, a bartering economy, would take our world back to what it was like in medieval times."

Her hand lifted to her mouth in surprise as a four-carat ring slowly spun on her thin finger, succumbing to gravity's inexorable pull. She mumbled that she thought it would be just fine with her, so Jakob continued.

"Imagine travel across the country to a protest taking weeks because no airlines can afford to buy new planes without debt." That got her attention, and she recoiled at the thought.

He went further. "Throughout history when debt markets have dried up, economies come to a screeching halt, and people's lives get worse. There are layoffs, bankruptcies, hiring stops, bonuses stop, and hours are cut. The global crash of 2008 was a debt crash. Banks got caught with worthless mortgages on their books and had to prove they could be solvent, or they risked being shuttered like Lehman Brothers. They stopped lending and called in debts. They raised their margin requirements, and the market crashed."

She was feeling garrulous and countered, "We would survive."

"You might survive, yes, but your store wouldn't. Expensive, rare books fall into the very unnecessary luxury category. Your Mercedes-Benz," he nodded out the window, "would have to go. The mortgage on your co-op would be called when the store closed, so then the apartment would be gone. Health care...gone. No job, no car, no apartment, no insurance. You would owe vendors for the stock seized when you didn't pay your business loan, and you would owe the bank for that loan as well. Your banks would hound you for repayment. How long would you enjoy life like that?"

Jakob paid cash for the book and left as she stared after him.

He knew the outburst was unnecessary. He didn't need to pop her gilded bubble. Still, he got agitated when someone living an extraordinary life, a life better than the lives of kings, felt somehow elevated by vilifying the system that enabled it.

As a banker, Jakob had helped the economies of Europe grow. He enabled hundreds of thousands of families to move beyond subsistence living. He was proud of that. Her pompous, poorly thought-out positions offended him.

If he was honest with himself, she wore far too much of her perfume, Lalique Soleil Crystal Extrait which sold for the price of a new car, and that probably compelled him to override his preference to ignore her.

*But back to my potential captors. I'm going to have to think my way out of my current predicament.*

153

# CHAPTER 24

# LIFE 10.0 -
# ROTHSCHILD PHOENIX 1769

J akob had a lot to do in a short amount of time for his bold, likely insane, strategy to work. First, he must figure out if becoming Rothschild was even workable, so he started by looking more closely at the body. Jakob still struggled to notice the details of people's faces and so he hadn't noticed that they looked about the same age. When Jakob stared at the corpse's face, and then his own reflection off a silver platter he'd picked up, he saw the similarity. Mayer had all his teeth, and Jakob had all of his. They had similar noses and, when Jakob bunched his eyebrows, he could see Mayer's intense stare in his reflection.

Rothschild's jacket, with the gold rings that identified the wearer as Jewish, was a good fit. Mayer's hair was longer than Jakob's, but on closer inspection, Jakob discovered Rothschild wore an unpowdered wig. Jews, he remembered, couldn't wear powdered wigs because of another of the ridiculous rules meant to suppress them. Jakob figured he could test the switch making no false claims and walked back to the front of the store, unlocking the front door.

While Jakob waited for another customer, he looked through Mayer's shop and found a diary, which he slipped into his pocket to read later. He then looked for letters or anything that could tell him about Mayer's personal life if the diary was actually a glorified sales ledger. Many people would be uncomfortable being near a dead body, but Jakob had been near hundreds of corpses in the last 300 years, and they did not bother him.

He heard a clatter of horses and a carriage coming to a stop outside the shop. Carriages were rare in the ghetto, and this belonged to none other than Crown Prince Wilhelm himself, who strode into the tiny shop, allowing the smell of the horse dung from the street to slip in.

*The intense smell is going to take some getting used to.*

Prince Wilhelm had just appointed Rothschild his Court Jew.

"Rothschild," Wilhelm said, "a Scandinavian friend has offered me an impressive collection of coins. I need to know what they're worth and if you can finance them."

"Do you have the coins with you?" Jakob asked, hoping it could buy him some time.

The prince dumped perhaps 200 coins on the silver platter Jakob had just used as a mirror. "The Scandinavian is in the carriage. I don't have long to decide."

Had it been clothing, art, horses, land, or almost anything else, Jakob would have been at a loss to come up with a quick valuation, but these were coins and Jakob knew money. He began quickly sorting them, expecting at any moment that Wilhelm would recognize Jakob wasn't Rothschild and set off an alarm, but the prince stood watching him sort. There were many duplicates, which simplified the valuation.

"These are worth twelve hundred gulden," Jakob told him minutes later. The gulden had replaced the florin decades before throughout the Holy Roman Empire of the German Nation.

"But he is asking seven thousand gulden!" the prince exclaimed, flustered.

"Then perhaps he is not as good a friend as you thought. There are twenty-four Roman Solidus Justinian II, which, if real, would make this worth seven thousand, but these are fake. On the real coins, you do not see a profile, but the full face of Justinian II."

Wilhelm's eyes went wide. He stormed out of the shop and over to his carriage. There was a vigorous but muffled exchange, and Wilhelm emerged a minute later, smiling.

"Rothschild, you are brilliant! I bought them for eleven hundred gulden! By the way, can you lend me..." the prince opened his purse and counted, "nine hundred twenty gulden?"

This was the deciding moment, and Jakob went for it. "Absolutely. I will have the money here at sunset."

"I am in your debt," the prince said, "quite literally." He laughed at his own joke as he returned to his carriage. "I will send my man at sunset."

The carriage drove off, too fast for the quality of the alley, splashing mud and manure on the houses as it passed. Jakob worried more about what to do with the body than about coming up with 920 gulden; he had that in his room in Frankfurt. He closed the shop early, that being Mayer's habit, and went into the back room. It was cluttered but everything was labeled in Hebrew. Jakob eventually found Rothschild's ledger book and looked through it. Rothschild was meticulous, good at accounting, and despite the Hebrew labels, he wrote it in German. This made it easier for Jakob to read. Jakob could read his financials as if he were reading Rothschild's biography printed on one of Herr Gutenberg's presses.

*I can do this.*

# CHAPTER 25

# LIFE 18.0 - AUGSBURG 2021

Before dawn, Bernthaler's crew positioned themselves around the grocery store. On the roof of a sporting goods store, one man watched from under a tarp that blended with the tiles. Another man crouched, nearly invisible, in the alley behind the store. A third man hid on the roof of the lighting store next to the grocery, secreted behind a tarp he'd painted to look like part of the air conditioner he crouched beside.

Bernthaler himself sat in the apartment above the grocery, which he'd secured for the week by paying three months' rent. There, he manned the six drones and coordinated with everyone on a radio. Jakob slipped in the back, past graffiti tags which made his jaw clench, and waited in the stockroom. He was too amped up to concentrate on anything or keep still, so he straightened and organized the stock to pass the time.

*If she keeps to her habits, the winking girl should arrive in half an hour. I'm not sure there is enough stock to accommodate my nervous energy.*

The Viktualien Feinkost grocery store that K. Weber went to each day tidily combined an organic grocery and delicatessen. Unlike the super-bright, massive American grocery stores, this was a small space with low wooden shelves lit primarily by the reflected light through the windows overlooking the street. From one corner, Jakob could see everyone standing in the store. Permeating the store was a light mix of the scents of lemon rind and tilled earth. Jakob loved the smell. As he finished organizing, an older woman in a yellow hat walked in, Jakob's signal that the winking girl would enter soon.

Moments later, the bells on the door rang, and it happened again. *It is her.*

He felt warm and weak and aroused and dumbstruck as their eyes met. She was stunningly beautiful with dark eyes, dark hair, and smooth, tanned skin. Slender and petite, she stood only 5' 1" and Jakob realized with relief that she looked about 28 years old. Gravity tugged him to her, and then she smiled.

That same dazzling smile.

Jakob's knees lost their strength, and he forgot hundreds of years of safety discipline. Without being aware of having moved, he found himself next to her. He took her hand and kissed her on the lips, as if they had been married for years. She looked surprised but did not pull back. "I see you, and I have been waiting for you," Jakob said.

She smiled and winked, and they both laughed as Jakob's hand slipped around her back as if it belonged there.

"It's so nice that you can talk this time because we have so much to discuss," she said, teasing him about their first meeting. Though he agreed, Jakob was happy just to be near her, as if mere proximity made the world a better place.

*I do not know why I am so at ease with her. I would never take another woman's hand, much less kiss her without explicit permission, but it is as if we belong together.*

In his mind, they were already married. Fraulein Weber seemed to feel the same sense of ease as she held his hand and looked into his eyes.

"We certainly do," he replied, still holding her. They walked through the few aisles of the store, paying no attention to the produce. After several minutes, the woman in the yellow hat passed in front of them, and it brought him back to the situation at hand.

He said, "I have a rather urgent question for you, and it will sound very odd. May I?"

"Please do," she smiled.

"Have you, by chance, hired teams of mercenaries to capture me?"

This was not what she expected, and she laughed out loud, "No. Why on earth would I go to that trouble when a simple five-letter email brought you around the globe to see me?"

Jakob smiled and kissed her again. "I'm so relieved to hear that. Unfortunately, someone has hired mercenaries, and they're targeting me."

"Oh, this is even more exciting than I expected." Her perfect eyebrows arched, but rather than looking apprehensive, she seemed invigorated. "I take it you are taking precautions?"

"Of course," he responded, nodding to the woman in the hat, who nodded back and then shifted her coat enough to reveal a small Walther PPK on her belt.

She giggled at that. It turned out that a 560-year-old woman giggling is unbelievably endearing. "This is splendid! Do we need to escape to a safe house, or something cloak and dagger like that?"

"By odd coincidence, we do! Are you able to leave right now?"

She gave a quick nod yes, then he took her hand and they walked across the street, where a Toyota Hilux pickup truck, a plumbing van, and a compact car all started simultaneously. Jakob walked with her to the plumbing van as its door slid open.

"A plumber's truck! You do know how to charm a lady!" she joked. The interior of the van had nothing to do with plumbing, as they'd outfitted it more like the interior of a private jet. The two settled in, releasing the fresh leather smell from the plush seating, and the three vehicles moved out, driving in a miniature convoy, but not close enough to draw attention. Inside the van, the two sat very close to one another.

"Okay, my turn for a question," she said. "What do I call you?"

"I have used many names over the last several centuries. My real name, as you know, is Jakob Fugger, and because I thought enough time had passed to reuse it, that's the name that I'm using now. *Quid pro quo*. What do I call you?"

"You can call me 'yours,'" she laughed at her own joke. "I'm using the name Kellyann Weber now, but I was born Anja Risacher. I was pretty sure you were my Jakob Fugger when I discovered you'd purchased $187,000 of burgundy. That's why I sent you the 'JF ICU.' But now it's my turn." She turned serious, and asked, "Why do you think we haven't died?"

"I don't know. I assume we were exposed to something in Augsburg around the time we met," Jakob replied.

She arched one eyebrow. "My theory is that it was the red wine at the festival where we met. I've thought about it for a long time," she smiled, "and you and I were the only two that drank the red wine in Frederick's box. I felt very odd for days afterward, and I thought it was because I'd fallen in love with you…which I had, by the way. While that may have contributed, I think someone poisoned the wine with something."

*She just said that she loved me.*

Intensely turned on, Jakob found it difficult to concentrate. "I remember everything from that meeting. One of Frederick's servants gave me a glass of red wine. I remember you coming at Frederick's beckoning. Your eyes, smile, hair, and wink are what I remember, though I recall being struck mute and paralyzed. Afterward, I felt heartsick and quite odd.

"I fell in love with you the moment I saw you, but I never connected the longevity to the wine," Jakob admitted, shaking his head, "because I thought others were drinking the wine."

*Had we honestly just said in passing that we were in love with one another?*

"Almost everyone was drinking, but only you and I had the red wine. I think someone tried to poison Frederick. He usually drank pinot noir, but he drank beer because of the heat. So only you and I had the red. Fortunately, we didn't drink enough to kill us, just enough for it to change our immune responses. The poison mixed with our high levels of oxytocin, in effect, vaccinated us against aging on a cellular level. I think if you check, you'll find you have few senescent cells, and your telomeres are long and robust. Senescent cells are those cells that should have died and had their nutrients reabsorbed, but instead they are sort of like zombie cells, no longer doing their job, instead just getting in the way. And telomeres are the markers at the ends of chromosomes that get shorter each time DNA replicates. When they get too short, the DNA will no longer replicate. I suspect you'll find that your telomeres are like those of a young man."

"Amazing. Do you have medical training?" Jakob asked, stunned that she had figured it out.

She hit him with a dazzling smile. "Jakob, I've had five and a half centuries to fill, so I've had training of all sorts."

He smiled back. "Point well taken. I want to know what you've been doing. I searched for you for decades in vain. Now that I've found you, I don't want to let you go, but I am possibly in real danger. I'm so terrible at these things," Jakob said, flustered, "Despite the danger, I don't want to be away from you. I love you. We should get married." Then, realizing what he had just blurted out, Jakob stopped, frozen.

"Oh, Jakob, we are definitely getting married. Have no fear of that. I've finally met a man that's older than me and a good kisser! No chance you're getting away." She took his hand in hers. "I have been bored for the last several centuries, so I am more than ready for an adventure. Tell me, who is chasing you and why?"

He started to speak, but stopped, pulled her into his arms, and kissed her, really kissed her. She tasted the way he imagined heroin felt like. He couldn't get enough. They must have kissed for ten minutes before he realized they were still in the van.

Slowly and almost painfully, Jakob pulled away from Kellyann and tried to regain his composure. "I'm sorry. I just couldn't wait for a second longer. What was your question?"

Composed, she responded, "Who is after you, and why?"

She seemed very amused at his physical discomfort and his futile attempts to obscure it with the van's leather pillows.

"Ah, right. I think someone is trying to capture me because they want to trade my money for my freedom. There is also circumstantial evidence that some very wealthy people are disappearing. I think it is because they've been targeted and want to avoid giving up much of their accumulated wealth. Given your wine buying habits, I'm guessing you're more than comfortable financially. Hopefully, they don't know about you."

"Or they didn't until we kissed in the grocery," she mentioned.

"Right." He realized just how dangerous was the game he'd drawn the woman he loved into. "As to who, I think it is someone with immense, governmental-level resources. They have tracked me to several locations across Europe and the USA, even after my taking significant security precautions."

"So, he's a billionaire? A dictator?" she asked.

"I think so, yes, probably Slavic, and I'm going to find out precisely who soon," he admitted.

"Why you?" she asked.

"It's unlikely that they know about what I've set aside from my past. But even in this life, I have accrued enough assets to draw some envious attention."

"Ah, so you're a billionaire, the same as whoever is after you?" She was blunt and accurate. There was no hint of awe or teasing in her question.

"Many times over," he admitted, equally bluntly.

"Well, that makes sense. You were a wizard at making money before." She paused for a moment, then asked, "You said 'excluding what you set aside in the past'?"

"Yes, I left almost everything I'd accumulated to my heirs and business partners when I 'died' and was 'reborn' under a different name." Jakob made air quotes around the words died and reborn. "But I put a small percentage of each life's accumulation in discrete accounts that have appreciated."

She lifted her eyebrows and smiled as she ran the calculations. "The compounding must be gargantuan after all this time."

She smiled again at his surprised expression. "I've also been investing for quite a while, Jakob. We both have compounding returns and compounding lives. So, how do you propose we stop this asshat who's after you?"

It was now his turn to smile, and he laid out his plan.

# CHAPTER 26

# LIFE 10.0 - JUDEN FRANKFURT 1770

J akob thought he understood the plight of the Jews in Europe when he became Mayer Rothschild, but he realized he'd had no idea. The ghetto where all the Frankfurt Jews were forced to live was called the Frankfurt *Judengasse*, or Jew Alley. It was a small U-shaped area outside the old city walls with buildings lining both sides and the end. Mud and manure made up the alley.

Jews couldn't leave Jew Alley except at specific times and for specific purposes. If a Christian were to yell at Jakob, "Jew, do your duty," he would have to step aside and remove his hat. Certain prognathic young boys seemed to delight in that when not pulling the wings off flies or hurting small animals. As a Jew, Jakob could not walk on the main street of Frankfurt, and the city permitted only fifteen marriages per year to take place in Jew Alley.

As Jakob awkwardly settled into Mayer's life, anger grew in him. Nobody suspected that the new Mayer Rothschild wasn't the same as the Mayer that had lived there the week before. Who would ever want to pretend to be a Jew in Frankfurt?

Christians would come begging for Jakob, as Rothschild, to buy something or lend them money. Even at their most obsequious, they would insult him in ways that would have been unthinkable if they'd known he was a Christian.

Jakob still believed in a God. He no longer thought God was an interventionist, moved by prayers or suffering to act, and he did not believe God would change anything because someone paid the pope for an indulgence. He could no longer believe God took an interest in limiting human suffering or eliminating cruelty. But Jakob believed in a power that created life. Jakob believed in the same God as the Christian men standing in the coin shop, who also unquestioningly believed that Jews killed children to sweeten bread with their blood and drank the urine of pigs.

Jakob did things differently in this life. Rather than focus on building his personal wealth, he would make his family so financially powerful that nobody would dare casually insult them. This would take time, planning, and a lot of work. Jakob's first wife, Sibylle, was a terrible match for him. His second wife, Edda, was a lovely and kind person and he enjoyed his life with her and loved her as a companion, partner, and mother of his children. The fact that he couldn't love her fully and that he couldn't change his son's decision to be a *Backpfeifengesicht*, which translated into "someone in need of a good face punch," hurt his heart. But someone like Edda was not who Jakob was searching for now.

To accomplish his new goal, Jakob knew he had to be very careful in his choice of bride, for she had to be intellectual and willing to fight to change the status quo. Despite being the son of a brilliant mother, he knew his decision to seek a brilliant wife was not driven by Oedipal tendencies, but by practicalities. For his sons to change how Europe treated Jews, his task would be much easier if they were very smart. His best shot at having intelligent children came from marrying a brilliant woman. Of course, for selfish reasons, he wanted her to be pretty and to like him.

It took time, but eventually, he met Guttle. Although she didn't have a name that rolled off the tongue, she was pretty, very smart, and had terrible taste in men. She found him both handsome and charming. She also struggled to tolerate the blatant discrimination against Jews.

"What makes me such a different woman from a Gentile?" she asked, seething after the city compelled them to postpone their planned wedding for three months because of the limit on Jewish marriages.

"Many things," Jakob said. "You are beautiful, intelligent, literate and you know mathematics. You speak several languages, value education, and you will succeed at what you put your mind to."

She couldn't hide her smile. "You know what I mean!"

"Yes, I do. To the degree they think of Jews, they are afraid of Jews. They cram us into a tight cage and have ridiculous restrictions, yet we thrive when so many in Germany do not. Can you imagine how anxious they would be if we didn't have restrictions?"

"I never thought of it that way," she replied. "They should be nervous because our children will compel them to lift those restrictions!"

"We will need to sacrifice to ensure our boys can do that," he replied. While he had a plan to tackle the injustice of Jewish discrimination, he knew he could not take on discrimination against women at the same time.

169

*That will come later.*

"Then we will sacrifice," she hissed with a dark stare off into the distance.

Jakob had been confident about it before, but at that moment, he was sure that she was the woman who would help him empower their children. Jakob had a mental image of his two sons conquering the world of merchants and banking. Unbeknownst to Jakob, Guttle planned to have as many more children and wasted no time.

Four months later, they were married. She'd reorganized the house and his coin shop, and she was pregnant.

# CHAPTER 27

# LIFE 18.0 -
# A DRIVE TO FRANCE 2021

After twenty minutes, the three-vehicle convoy pulled into a dark warehouse in the small town of Berkheim, Germany. Jakob and Kellyann stayed in the van while Bernthaler's men replaced the German plumbing signage on the van with that of a French florist, resplendent in pinks and yellows. They also changed the plates. But, more important to its occupants, Bernthaler's men had sandwiches and drinks waiting, including a superb, chilled Grand Cru Burgundy from Domaine Meo-Camuzet Richebourg.

They decided to keep driving to get out of Germany. Once they'd picked a destination, Jakob knew they'd have about seven hours to talk once the van pulled away. And so, they talked for seven hours.

He told Kellyann about his lives and discovered she'd also recreated herself many times over. He discovered she knew about his Life 1.0 as Jakob Fugger. She knew about his wife, businesses, and mines, wealth, and the indulgences.

Jakob told her about farming, selling tulips, the Dutch East India Company, and his inability to turn around his son in the Netherlands. He told her about taking over Rothschild's life, which didn't surprise her as much as he'd expected, and his goal to improve the lives of European Jews.

She told him about her arranged marriage to a coarse man about two months after she met Jakob for the first time and how she lived in fear of his temper and drinking. Jakob learned about the handmaid he'd hired for her, who looked like her sister. She told him how the handmaid died after Kellyann's husband had raped her and poisoned her for getting pregnant. Kellyann explained how she had pretended to have ingested some poison and faked her own death, escaping the marriage and starting a new life.

She told him about where she'd lived, and how she'd never been able to have children. How, in fact, she'd never been able to love a man fully. How she'd moved to America in the seventeenth century and lived in New Amsterdam for years before they renamed it New York. She revealed her investments in the Dutch West India Company, which she'd had to make through a proxy, and how she'd sold it once she discovered it was involved in the slave trade. Kellyann talked about living in Ireland, Czarist Russia, Malta, small islands in the Pacific, and Scandinavia. She'd even lived in Turkish Constantinople, which is now called Istanbul.

When they took a break to eat, Jakob confessed his responsibility for the religious wars. She had lived through all the wars between the Protestants and Catholics and was surprised to discover that he blamed himself for triggering them.

"But Jakob, you didn't start them. You didn't fund them or support them. So, they are not your fault," she reasoned.

"While that is true, I agreed to take the money from the indulgences that led Luther to call out the Vatican, which then led to a schism in the Church, then the wars," he responded.

"If you had refused to take the money from the indulgences, what would have happened?" she asked. He'd never thought of that.

"If I'd refused, they would have used my refusal as a reason for Albrecht not to repay the loan."

"Would they have issued the indulgences, anyway?" Her question was simple and simply immense.

Jakob had blamed himself for the needless deaths brought about by the Catholic-Protestant conflicts, from the first death through the Troubles in Northern Ireland. He held himself responsible for tens of millions of deaths. But Kellyann was right. They would have issued the indulgences anyway.

Jakob had influence, yes, but not enough to make Pope Leo X pass up such easy money. Nothing he could have said or done would have made any difference to the pope or the archbishop once they had that money in their sight.

"Yes, they would have issued the indulgences anyway," he replied almost silently, and he felt the weight of millions of deaths lift at that moment.

Then, to Kellyann's and Jakob's great surprise, he began to cry. Five hundred years of guilt for millions of deaths evaporating led, not to a single manly tear streaking down Jakob's stoic cheek, but to a full-on, nose-running, body-shaking blubbering.

To her credit, Kellyann said nothing and just held him. Although he cried like a baby, Jakob felt better at that moment than he had ever felt. He was with the girl of his dreams, literally, and she had just absolved him of a massive crime he thought he had committed.

When his blubbering stopped, he explained to her what had just happened, and again to their joint surprise, Kellyann cried. He just held her. Luckily, there were lots of tissues in the van.

They agreed to move on to lighter subjects and talked about wine and burgundy in particular. She told him she had been a vigneron in one of her past lives and grew pinot noir grapes on the Beaune River in France. That had always been a dream of Jakob's, but his inability to keep even potted flowers alive for more than a week disqualified him from pursuing it.

He told her about his love of sunsets, which sounded to him a bit like admitting he liked unicorns when he said it aloud. Fortunately for him, she didn't break into hysterics. Instead, she told him about her love of starling murmurations, where the birds fly in tightly coordinated flocks, swooping and turning as if they were part of a larger hive mind. Although Jakob was fascinated by murmurations, he didn't admit to it to avoid sounding like he loved all the things that she loved.

Jakob told her about his mines and how he'd secreted tons of gold hidden as radioactive waste. She thought it quite clever, which pleased him.

Kellyann then admitted that she created her own church in America. She explained she had the same compounding return problem that Jakob did after becoming a skilled investor, and that securing private assets that were growing ever more extensive had become exceptionally challenging. So, she formed a church.

"Are you religious?" he asked.

"Oh," she smiled, "not for hundreds of years. But the laws surrounding churches in the USA are ridiculous. They provide a type of financial insurance and give me a degree of privacy I could not replicate anywhere else in the world. The American IRS is very nervous about questioning churches. That is how the evangelical TV ministers get away with using donations for their mansions and multiple jets. Whereas my church only uses my money, does no harm, and does quite a bit of good."

"That is brilliant! What is your church's name?" he asked innocently.

She blushed so furiously that he thought she was choking, then she admitted it was called the "Seeking J." Church. Jakob's response was inappropriate for the topic, as he grew instantly aroused. He then blushed, and she tried not to smile.

They finished the filet mignon sandwiches, and Jakob poured the wine. As he prepared to toast, she beat him to it: "To the luck and skill we'll need to figure out how to use what we have to help people…once we get married."

*I really love her.*

After almost exactly seven hours, they arrived in a small French town in the Savoy region, just south of Geneva. The town was Annecy, on Lake Annecy, which is surrounded by mountains peppered with castles. Canals run through the old part of the town, making it look like a smaller, cleaner version of Venice. Swans, rather than gondolas, crowded the canals. It was one of Jakob's favorite places in the world, even if the swans were pretty mean.

CHAPTER 28

# LIFE 10.0 -
# KINDERMACHT FRANKFURT 1770

Jakob knew how he did what he did. He gathered information, gleaned it to find opportunities, and then converted opportunities into money.

However, he did not know at all how his wife, Guttle, did what she did. They had ten children. There was an even split between girls and boys. She raised and took care of all ten in their apartment, spacious by Judengasse standards, but cramped by almost any other standard. She did all this while pregnant or nursing year after year.

Five boys slept in one small room, five girls in another. Jakob had one room for the Rothschild coin trade. They had a kitchen and a little bedroom for Jakob and Guttle.

She fed, cleaned, raised, taught, and tended ten kids and Jakob. Guttle also took charge of the family's spiritual learning. She was proud to be Jewish, and she raised the Rothschild children with that same pride.

By comparison, Jakob had only two jobs. The first was to make money, and the second was to teach the boys business and how to make money. Wealth would be the key that got them out of the ghetto.

From the time they were small children, Jakob and his sons played the game of *geschäft*, or business. The *geschäft* questions started simply but got more complex the older they grew. Jakob would describe a situation, and the boys would puzzle it out together.

"Amschel is a cloth dealer," he would start when the kids were young, "what does he buy, what does he sell, and who does he pay?" After the teasing about Amschel being a rag dealer calmed down, they worked to answer the question.

As they aged, the questions got harder. "There are three things that cloth dealer James can do to make three different levels of profit. What are they?"

Access to current and accurate information was vital to making money, so the lessons also focused on getting information. "Nathan is at a social event where he meets the butler of the Bank of England's director. What should he do?"

Each of the five boys had suggestions, and they were all similar. "Bring him into our employ to keep us informed of what is going on at the bank."

Jakob also stressed that the speed of information, getting it before others, was key. So, they strategized about how to do that. By far, the most popular idea was Nathan's plan to keep racehorses in Jew Alley. But they deemed it impractical after nobody would volunteer to feed or clean up after the horses. Second on the list was keeping homing pigeons; the pigeons were not dismissed out of hand.

By the time they were older, the questions in the game *geschäft* had grown more nuanced. "Amschel lives in Frankfurt, Carl and James in France, Nathan in England, and Solomon in the Netherlands. Each deals in government bonds and currency. But the markets are inefficient. A British coin in England is worth twenty percent more than the same British coin in France. A Dutch gulden in Germany is half the value of a Dutch gulden in France. What are the opportunities?"

Guttle became the perfect assistant professor. When Nathan would figure out a solution to a problem, she would praise him. If Solomon or Carl got confused, she would ask them leading questions until they understood. James, the youngest, would sit in her lap and talk capably about currency exchanges.

"Carl receives word through our network that the Germans have won a battle in Poland. What do you do?" Jakob asked, and each of them laid out their strategy to trade on the information. All of them were excellent strategies.

"So, what could you do to make it even better?" Jakob followed up.

Only Nathan wasn't stumped. On the contrary, he smiled, and was proud of his plan, and he announced, "I would go to the exchange and start selling German bonds," he said.

His brothers, hoping to win a strategy competition against Nathan finally, all stood and yelled, "Why would you sell German bonds? They will go up. Germany won the battle! Your trade is backward!"

Nathan sat still in the face of this barrage, and continued, "The price of the German bonds will initially fall because our network of informants will be well known, and so others will mimic our trades, sure we have better information. Then, when the price falls, I will buy German bonds on the cheap."

Nathan sat in Jakob's seat at the head of the table for dinner that night, which pleased him a great deal.

Guttle and Jakob, who had settled into his life as Mayer Rothschild, struggled with how they could keep five boys, who constantly fought one another, together in a unified business. One day, after Jakob's attempts at persuasion resulted in only minimal effect on brotherly unity, Guttle assured him she would handle it.

Later that week, she showed up with six arrows. Carl immediately cut himself on one, but rather than bandage him, she ignored the dripping blood and set one arrow on the table and bound the five other arrows together with a ribbon, setting them next to the single arrow.

"Who can break this arrow in half?" she asked, pointing to the single arrow.

After a lifetime of not being able to break anything in the apartment, the boys had an opportunity to break something, so they scrambled for the sole arrow. In the scuffle, Amschel and Solomon both managed to cut themselves. James ended up with it and smashed it across his knee, breaking it, and then he cut himself.

"Very good," she said, with four of her sons bleeding. "Does anyone else think they could also break it?" All four of the boys asserted they could break it in a far superior manner to what James had used. While trying to convince his mother of his arrow-breaking prowess, Amschel cut himself again. Once again, Guttle ignored the blood dripping all over her kitchen. Their daughters watched this bizarre bloodbath from their room, eyes wide.

Guttle quieted the boys and said, "And this bundle of five arrows, can anyone break this?" Amschel, the oldest, had anticipated the challenge and grabbed the bundle before anyone else and smashed it across his knee. He fell to the floor, writhing in pain and grabbing his knee as he covered himself in the blood pooled there. The bundled arrows rolled away intact.

She picked up the bundle and continued, "You can't break the five arrows when they are together! Remember that! The five arrows are like the five of you. If you stand alone, you can, and will, be broken! But standing together, nobody can break you." She then bent down and tended to Amschel's bruised leg. "You will never all agree on everything but let nothing separate you."

Finally, she took the broken arrow and cut Nathan's hand to his wide-eyed astonishment. She then cut Jakob's and her own, and together they all swore on the five arrows they would work together—a blood oath.

That night in bed, Jakob asked her how she found such razor-sharp arrows. She admitted she sharpened them to ensure they never forgot this lesson. "There is nothing quite like seeing your own blood to make you remember something important."

She was pretty sharp herself.

When he looked back on it, Jakob realized that his games of geschäft helped with the boy's future success, but it was likely that Guttle's arrow lesson made the larger difference. As the boys grew to men, Jakob laid out his plan for them.

"Each of you is like an arrow and will shoot into a distinct part of Europe. There, you will trade and eventually establish banks. You will communicate with each other many times each week, in code, and strengthen your intelligence collection and the speed of letter delivery in each location."

The lessons grew complex and real world, but the differences in the boys' ages made it challenging to develop one description that worked for all of them. For example, one evening, he was getting nowhere while attempting to explain the difference between being paid and making money through equity ownership. Guttle walked in on Jakob's sixth or seventh attempt and said to the younger boys in passing, "You are not rewarded for doing your job. You are paid for doing your job. You are rewarded for taking risks and initiative and owning something."

There were five sets of accusatory eyes as she walked out, wondering why Jakob hadn't just said it that way to start with.

Nathan was the smartest of the boys, but ironically, not the smartest of the children. Two of his sisters were brilliant in everything they did. Nathan took to strategy naturally. Unfortunately, like Jakob, he was a savant, brilliant at strategy and commerce, but clueless when dealing with people, feelings, emotions, or social niceties. More unfortunately, Nathan's inability to see social nuance was more pronounced than his father's.

Nathan showed fantastic skill with finance and trade, but keeping neat books fell far outside of his skill set. After lessons where he knew Jakob judged him on his clean bookkeeping, his bookkeeping was still sloppy, with parts of it missing. As smart as he was, he couldn't move it from head to paper without mistakes. He saw it correctly in his head, but on paper, it came out a mess. Social niceties made no sense to him. Part of his mind was crystalline. Every thought about business was clear. Almost everything else, from his language skills to his handwriting, was a disaster. Jakob pushed him to get a bookkeeper for decades, but with no success. Were Nathan subject to analysis today, Jakob was confident doctors would diagnose him with Asperger's Syndrome.

Shortly after Jakob had laid out the family strategy, Nathan, the English arrow, shot himself off to England.

James, the youngest, couldn't wait to get to France and left at the first opportunity to study. Solomon and Carl stayed in Frankfurt, but over time they went to Naples and Vienna, while Amschel stayed in Frankfurt.

# CHAPTER 29

# LIFE 18.0 -
# ANNECY FRANCE 2021

J akob slept in for the first time in centuries.

The evening before, he and Kellyann had arrived at his house on Lake Annecy, which sits one kilometer outside the historic town of Annecy, on the way to Talloires. They arrived in time for a sunset dinner and drank two bottles of the 2004 Romanée-Conti Echezeaux that Jakob had in his cellar.

With everything that happened the previous day, enjoying a glass of excellent wine with the woman he loved while watching the sunset was sublime. It paled compared to what happened in the six hours after they finished the wine and went to bed.

Before falling asleep, the last thing Jakob remembered was saying, "Wow, you make me feel like I'm 100 again," and then Kellyann punched him in the arm.

The sun had been up for hours, glinting on the ripples in the lake when Jakob awoke, knowing he had to email the Romanians, or the clock would start ticking with nothing for them to do. Their hourly rate was eye-watering, so he headed down to his office and got to work.

Hello my friend, I'm pleased to be working together again. While I'd like to implement something like a targeted NotPetya, I am not positive who should benefit from its attention. Therefore, I would appreciate your help with the following questions:

- Someone is stalking and attempting to capture me and other Ultra High Net Worth individuals. Who is it?
- My primary accounts are in Goldman Sachs, Merrill/ Bank of America, Wells Fargo, Rothschilds, and Banco do Brasil. Can you see if someone is sniffing around them, and if so, who? I won't insult you by providing account numbers.
- Where are the assets held by whoever is after me, and can we put them at risk?
- If we must use a show of power by emptying an account, which is the best account for a demonstration?
- Is there a more effective pressure point we can use?
- How many UHNWIs are they targeting?
- Once we convince them to stop, what can we do to ensure they stay stopped?

As always, I appreciate your help.

When he emerged from his office, Kellyann was moving around the kitchen, looking radiant.

"Did you send the email?" she asked with a smile that increased his heart rate. Jakob nodded and then took her in his arms and kissed her.

Breakfast on the grass overlooking the lake tasted delicious. The day was warm with a breeze that came off the lake, making the temperature perfect. The castles were barely visible through a morning mist, and a few of the canal swans glided across the lake surface, but the discussion turned to business. She started right away, "What are your priorities?"

"My highest priority is keeping you safe. After that, I want to stop whoever is trying to capture me, and maybe us. After that, marrying you is high on my list, followed by figuring out how we help people."

She grinned at that, but then got serious again. "What are your next steps to stop whichever former Soviet asshat is trying to capture you?"

"I just engaged the Romanian hacking team. Once we know for sure who is doing this, I want to put a squeeze on their assets, so, at the very least, we reach a state of Mutually Assured Destruction."

"Nobody but me knows about your buried gold?" she asked.

"Just you, and one highly incentivized manager in the mine," he responded. "Now, my turn, what are your priorities?"

"First, I want to help you shut down any attempt to kidnap you. I'm not anxious about my safety because I've proven quite hard to kill, so don't worry overmuch about me. Then, we should get married and help people. After that, I have two other minor objectives once things slow down."

"Okay…" He paused, waiting for her to continue, but she stayed silent. "What are the minor objectives?"

"I don't intend to sound mean, but we need to improve your wardrobe and the design choices for your houses if they look like this one. Do your other houses look like this?"

He was shocked. "More or less, yes, but I want to keep a low profile. I don't want large, flashy houses."

"A low profile is smart, but my love, you dress as if you walked out of JC Penney's catalog in 1992. And this house could be so charming, but it looks like it was last decorated in the 1970s. When did you last update it?"

He couldn't hide his embarrassed smile. "Ummm, in 1972. Is it that bad?"

"Honestly, that style is so out of fashion it is coming back. Don't worry about it. I will take care of it. Or should I say, 'them'? How many houses have you decorated like the Brady Bunch's?"

"I'm not sure who the Bradys are, but I have fourteen houses. I don't trust hotel security."

She laughed, "I have eight."

"Nice…where are your eight?"

"Well, you know about the house in Augsburg," she replied. "I also have houses in San Francisco, Rarotonga in the Cook Islands, Grand Cayman, Geneva, Athens, Vancouver, and Menton."

"I love your choices. Everything is near water! The Cook Islands are outstanding. I tried to get a house there, but I was told I couldn't own land there because I'm not a Cook Islander."

"True," she said, "but because I owned a business there, I could buy a house."

After comparing the locations of their houses, they cleaned up and took a very hot shower together. Even in his distracted state, Jakob noticed for the first time that the color of the tile in the master bathroom was olive green.

Once they dressed, they walked into the old city, wandering aimlessly across bridges and through the narrow streets. They stopped at a clothing store, and Jakob realized the wandering may have been not aimless. Leaving the store an hour later, he wore jeans made with stretchy denim that proved to be ridiculously comfortable, and he carried three bags of clothes.

After a light lunch, they descended to Jakob's office, which was snug for two people, and he checked email because the Romanians worked fast. They put dozens of hackers on a project. Their reply was brief and to the point.

Hello Friend, the clock has started ticking, so here are your answers.

- Who? Alexander Lukashenko.
- Who's sniffing your accounts? An ex-FancyBear leads his cyber team, and that team is sniffing at these accounts and your Vanguard, Schwab, and RBC accounts. The would-be kidnappers are being funded and led by the State Security Committee of the Republic of Belarus.
- His assets? He has over three billion US dollars split among his accounts at Paritet Bank, Belarusbank, and about $900 million in an e-Trade account.
- Where for a demonstration? Belarusbank's security is a joke. We can start there.
- Other pressure points? He has three sons, Nikolai, Dimitri, and Viktor. Each has eight-figure accounts at Paritet Bank.
- How many billionaires were targeted? Sixteen. Each is worth at least $3 billion, but none worth more than $150 billion, except you, but it is unlikely they know that. Seven of the sixteen are off the grid.

- Ongoing protection? We can handle that. I won't specify how. It will cost $40 million. Non-negotiable.

Enjoy the lake and update your VPN!

A sense of relief washed over Jakob despite the hackers making it clear they knew his location and that he had other accounts he hadn't disclosed. FancyBear, the top Russian hacking team that works for Putin, had hackers as good as or possibly better than the Romanians.

Kellyann read over his shoulder, "Lukashenko. Thank goodness!"

"Right? I was worried it was Putin," Jakob replied.

"Better a warthog than a cobra," she said.

Jakob then shook his head as his VPN generated a pop-up, asking if he wanted to update it.

"Superb hackers are scary," he said as he clicked to install the update.

CHAPTER 30

# LIFE 10.0 -
# FIVE ARROWS EUROPE 1798

The young Rothschilds went out into the world and into business. At Guttle's suggestion, they worked for a while with no guidance. Nathan, ironically, got involved in the cloth trade in England, and after a few disappointments, grew his business. James continued his education in France and soon became the most formally educated of all his brothers. Jakob had to warn him that France taxed on apparent wealth, not actual wealth, so he should live modestly until a more lavish lifestyle became unavoidable.

Amschel stayed around Frankfurt and worked to grow the business while Solomon moved to Vienna and Carl to Naples. The five arrows were now all in different parts of Europe, and though they were working independently at first, they stayed very close.

Over the past many years, Jakob, as Mayer Rothschild, sold coins to the Crown Prince Wilhelm of Hesse at just below his cost, and that investment finally paid off. The revolution in France had all the regents of Europe on edge, and Wilhelm wanted to borrow. The Rothschilds were ready for him.

Jakob and his sons had grown their Frankfurt business, and they could handle Wilhelm's loan with ease. As they had hoped, additional loans from other princes, landgraves, kings, and governments followed, which positioned them well to get into bond issues. Working together, the five arrows of Rothschild arbitraged currency exchange rates, and soon each of them had significant books of business.

Nathan took an early leadership position over his brothers and gave them orders rather than requests. Much to their annoyance, his ideas worked out well, but his tone was authoritarian. Jakob let his boys work it out despite the stress it put on the family. Jakob's next responsibility, as he saw it, was to improve the speed of their information network.

The fastest similar networks were the diplomatic ones. Diplomats could reliably get information from Austria to England in a week, and occasionally in only six days, if ships were ready at the English Channel. A week wouldn't do, so the Rothschilds invested in homing pigeons and kept the fastest ships on retainer. The brothers developed contacts at the banks, government, shippers, and everywhere from warehouses to whorehouses—anywhere that could get them reliable information. They started using color-coded envelopes that could show at a glance whether interest rates were up or down in the sender's location and whether to buy or sell. Soon, they could get information from Austria to England reliably in three days.

News of the speed of the Rothschild network slipped out, and soon, their networks were carrying messages for regents throughout Europe. Although they wouldn't breach a royal seal, knowing who the government was secretly contacting turned out to be an additional source of valuable information.

192

Having news before others proved invaluable in dozens of deals, which allowed the boys to double their assets. But the most public use of it came from Nathan. He had developed a habit of going to the Bourse, London's financial exchange, and leaning against a pillar. Couriers and brokers would approach him one after the other to give information or quickly make proposals he would agree to or dismiss. Thus, he earned the nickname "The Pillar of the Bourse." He also became the acknowledged pillar of the family, with the other brothers eventually agreeing to follow his lead.

Napoleon had been conquering parts of Europe for France for years, and he was now fighting the British, Prussians, and the Dutch near the village of Waterloo in Belgium, a British territory in 1798. Everyone expected Napoleon would win, and a win at Waterloo for Napoleon would change the face and fate of Europe.

The Rothschild high-speed network got word to Nathan that Napoleon had lost. Nathan then went to the Bourse and began selling British bonds, leaning against his pillar, with no expression on his face. Soon the word spread that Rothschild was selling, and everyone began dumping British bonds. Once the price fell, Nathan and the league of brokers trading on his behalf, bought at the reduced price. He had used the exact strategy he came up with years before at the dinner table in the Judengasse. The millions of pounds of profit cemented his reputation, and he earned a new moniker, "The Investor of London."

Under Nathan's and Jakob's guidance, the other Rothschild sons built their businesses until individually they controlled top banks in their markets. Together, as the five arrows, they were unmatched. Kings and princes consulted them regularly. They worked together as a force for peace and stability in Europe when there was massive turmoil.

Before Jakob, pretending to age as Mayer Rothschild, "died," he passed his ultimate aim to his sons. "You have attained great financial positions in your respective countries. Use those positions to improve the situation of Jews across Europe. Get the laws changed and limits removed."

Overcoming the structural bigotry against Jews would be difficult, but they dedicated themselves to it. Mayer Rothschild had been made a baron and, though he chose not to use the title, his sons made good use of it and the other titles they accumulated. England, Austria, Germany, Italy, and France soon found Rothschilds at the top of their business, social, and eventually, their governmental ranks.

The Rothschilds had country estates, royal titles, and held the most coveted balls. As an association with the Rothschilds became a sought-after position, the restrictions against Jews fell away. A Rothschild sat in Parliament. Prejudice still existed, but it was no longer brazenly embodied in the law. With great pride, Jakob could say the five arrows of Rothschild and their children helped break the legacy of institutionalized discrimination against Jews.

CHAPTER 31

# LIFE 18.0 -
# CHEZ ENFANTS 2021

After three days of preparation, it was time to deal with Alexander Lukashenko, the brutal President of Belarus, and its dictator. The asshat (Jakob's new favorite word courtesy of Kellyann) was trying to steal money from Jakob and others. Trained as a Soviet farmer, he lacked even the minimal subtlety of Putin, his political hero. But his willingness to demolish any dissent made subtlety less important.

The Romanians had provided Lukashenko's personal cell phone number. With the help of Bernthaler, Jakob had spoofed two burner phones so the calls would appear to come from the head of the Belarus State Security Committee. Jakob's Russian was passable but rusty, but Kellyann was fluent, and after three minutes of arguing about who would make the call, they settled it like professionals. Jakob chose scissors and lost to her rock.

At 11:30 p.m. Belarus time, 10:30 p.m. Annecy time, she called Lukashenko.

"Gregor, it is late. What the hell is so important?" Lukashenko sounded groggy, annoyed, and drunk.

*Good.*

"Alyaksandar, I now have control of your money and the money of your sons." Her Russian was flawless, and she used a slight Belarusian accent. A nice touch. "Don't hang up, or I will make it disappear. Do not—"

His outburst interrupted her. "Who is this? Do you know who you are dealing with? You..." He was apoplectic. Jakob and Kellyann smiled at one another.

She interrupted him. "Shut up, Alyaksandar. You just cost yourself one billion rubles with that little outburst. Go to your computer and check your account ending in 523 in Belarusbank. You have sixty seconds to come back, or another one billion rubles will go away." While a Belarus ruble was worth about only forty US cents, it was still a lot of money.

Lukashenko returned in forty-nine seconds, sounding deflated. "What have you done?" They could hear him gesticulating in the background, banging his hands on a desk or table.

"We have corrupted the accounts with a virus that will transfer the money to charities across the world. You just helped some needy children, perhaps the first nice thing you've done in decades. All of your accounts, and those of Nikolai, Dimitri, and Viktor, are compromised. The money will disappear if you try to move it. If you, or any of your men in the room with you now, try to trace the virus, it will disappear. If you keep up your attempt to kidnap the sixteen, it will disappear. Do you need more of your funds to evaporate before you believe me?" Jakob was in awe. She was such a badass.

"You will die for this."

*The bully's last stand we'd expected.*

196

"You just lost half of Dimitri's account at Paritet Bank." Two minutes and twenty-one seconds into the call, she hung up.

She switched to the other burner phone they'd prepared and called again as Jakob dismembered the first phone and dropped it in a glass of Diet Coke.

"Stop! Stop. Taking. My. Money!" he cried as he answered.

She scoffed. "We both know it is not 'your' money. Immediately end your kidnap program or your other accounts will be emptied. You may take out only one million rubles a week or your accounts will be emptied. If you screw this up, word will leak that you are penniless and powerless. Do you understand the implications of that?"

"Stop! Stop! Okay, everything will stop!" he screamed into the phone. Lukashenko wailed in frustration.

"Sleep well, Alyaksandar. By the way, that top makes you look fatter than usual." She hung up.

Jakob cocked an eyebrow, to which she responded, "What? We know he had others in the room. Even he wouldn't do that naked. Now he thinks we had eyes on him. He'll waste a week looking for cameras."

Jakob grinned from ear to ear as he dunked the second disabled phone. Then he took her hand, and they walked out of the house to the waiting van. Bernthaler's men had changed the van's license plate and hundreds of bland-looking nuts and bolts covering its side under the name of an Italian hardware distributor. The ride to her house in Port de Bellerive on Lake Geneva was only an hour, but with the privacy screen up, they made the most of it.

He realized she had great taste when he woke up the next morning. Nothing in her bedroom was flashy or over-the-top, but everything looked clean and felt welcoming. He tried to get out of bed without waking her, with no success.

"Good morning, my love." He kissed her lips lightly.

She held his arm for a moment. "Morning. You should check the news."

"That is first on my morning agenda, followed by getting you coffee," he told her. "Can I use your hard-wired computer?" He could hear the beeping of her coffee machine finishing its brew coming from her kitchen.

"Feel free. The password is A E one zero U."

*Of course it was.*

The internet was ablaze with speculation about who was behind the anonymous donations of US $10 million to more than four dozen children's charities overnight. Talking heads speculated that it may total over US $700 million. The German press had dubbed it KinderNacht, Children's Night. The French press now called its orphanages, Chez Enfants Riches, the Houses of Rich Kids. In Columbia, the press now called orphans, "Los Huérfanos de Beverly Hills," the Beverly Hills Orphans.

Jakob carried a cup of coffee into the bedroom and shared the news. "We just got two birds with one stone. We stopped Lukashenko, and we helped children. Not a bad night's work. But, to achieve that, we poked a hornet's nest. We have to be very cautious now."

# CHAPTER 32

# LIFE 13.0 -
# HISPANIOLA 1844

After spending some time in the new United States of America, under the pseudonym Santiago Nuevo, Jakob discovered the joys of sailing and the beauty of the Caribbean. He navigated around the islands there and settled on the eastern end of Hispaniola. The island was one of the few in the world that had, and still has, two different countries splitting it. On the west was French-influenced Haiti, while the east was the Spanish-influenced Dominican Republic.

The Dominicans had just won a war of independence from the Haitians, who had ruled over them for two generations. Even before the war, the people were poor; when Jakob arrived there, abject poverty was rampant, but it was mixed with pride and a strong work ethic.

Columbus had landed on the island in 1492 and found the natives wearing gold jewelry. The natives no doubt wore it to impress the strangers from the large boats, but it proved a most unfortunate decision for them, because Columbus and his Spanish backers were desperate for gold.

The Spanish search for gold and the diseases carried by the Spanish sailors wiped out millions of *Taíno* Indians on Hispaniola. The Indians had no resistance to diseases like smallpox that the Europeans had become effectively immune to. The Spanish discovered a gold vein, and they forced tens of thousands of Taíno down into the mines, never to climb back out.

This pointless death infuriated Jakob, who had owned mines, and while his mines were far from comfortable, almost all the miners that entered his mines came back out. It was ridiculous not to feed miners, a tragic and cruel waste of life. As the Taíno Indians died, the Spaniards brought African slaves to the island to continue searching for gold and to harvest the sugarcane they brought to the island once the easy-to-find gold was depleted.

Hispaniola's land was beautiful, as were its people. The Haitians spoke French, the Dominicans Spanish. Jakob spoke both fluently. After sailing around the island, he decided on a strategy that might help the islanders. He would make small loans and provide some basic economic suggestions to the people borrowing from him. So, as Jakob Nuevo, he sailed from port to port, making loans and collecting on the ones he had previously made.

The Dominicans proved to be diligent in their repayment. If they could not pay in currency, they would offer something in trade. Frequently, the offerings weren't something Jakob could use on a sailing ship, like livestock. He appreciated the effort.

One farmer offered Jakob a piglet but having grown up with pigs which only start out cute, Jakob refused. The piglet, however, would not accept his refusal, and it followed him around for weeks. Jakob nicknamed him Gordito. When he had to sail to the next inlet, Jakob left funds for an islander to raise Gordito with little doubt he would become quite successful with girl pigs.

If a Haitian didn't pay, and Jakob went to the local magistrate, the magistrate demanded a bribe to have him do his job. As they were common in the 1500s, Jakob understood bribes, but the Haitians demanded almost all the proceeds, which Jakob found outrageous. After losing control of the Dominican Republic, the Haitian government seemed focused on the infighting between the mulattos and the blacks. Government changes were frequent and depended largely on that single issue. Little governing was done, and corruption was rampant.

The Haitians were only slightly better off than the Dominicans, yet Jakob found their government unworkable. It proved an obstacle that Jakob could find no way to overcome without hiring his own small army of enforcers. He reluctantly wrote off dozens of his loans in Haiti and focused on the eastern half of the island. His goal was to help, not get robbed.

Working just the Dominican half of the island, Jakob found his small loans were so popular that he needed representatives in each region. So, he gathered ten men who'd proven trustworthy and had them meet him in the small mountain town of Bonao, in the center of the country. There, Jakob held a fifteen-day school on how to be a broker.

The first day, men showed up late and drunk and barely paid attention. He gave a silver coin to each man who arrived on time and sober. By the second day, nine men arrived sober and on time, but the tenth was late and drunk. The group had gathered enough attention that a circle of men formed around them, hoping to replace one of the ten. Jakob replaced the drunk tenth man, and from that point on, everyone showed up early and was sober.

Jakob taught them the basics of lending and investing and made his expectations clear. When he showed up in an area, he expected the broker to meet him and to have collected any money owed to Jakob. Further, he wanted the broker to preview for him who he would meet over the next two days and why they wanted the loans.

It took three months before things were running somewhat smoothly. Jakob's first meetings with borrowers were painful. They didn't know what they had, what they wanted, what they would do with the money, or when they could pay it back. So, he had the brokers coach them on how to apply for a loan, with the promise that Jakob would double the commission on any approved loan where the application was clear and well thought out.

# CHAPTER 33

# LIFE 18.0 - PLAKA 2021

Recognizing that Lukashenko's hackers were still out there and probably highly incentivized to find them, Jakob and Kellyann moved frequently. They were cautious with their phone and internet usage and kept a very low profile.

After a few weeks of moving around, they arrived at Kellyann's beautiful house in Athens that overlooked the Plaka. The Plaka is the ancient part of the city and has narrow roads filled with small shops, and an open market that has been there for hundreds of years. Like Kellyann's Geneva house, this house was small but so tastefully decorated that it felt spacious. From the exterior lighting to the bathroom sinks, everything worked together. Jakob walked the first floor evaluating the colors, carpet, and furniture, trying to figure out what made everything look good. He concluded her taste was like music. He could tell if it was good, but he was not capable of making wonderful music.

Kellyann was walking up to the bedroom ahead of him when the sound of screeching brakes and a car crash came from outside. A man screamed for help and, without thinking, Jakob ran out the front door to offer help because the accident was on the street only three blocks down from her house.

As he approached the scene of the accident, he could see that two older Fiats had smashed into each other head on. One of them was on fire. People were gathering around, and he asked an older woman in a headscarf if the drivers were okay. It had been at least a century since he'd spoken Greek, but she understood and responded in simple terms given his poor pronunciation, "No drivers. Nobody is here." Parts of the car, like the roof and trunk, were on fire.

*They shouldn't burn. Something is wrong with the scene. The cars are old and inexpensive. Nooo! This is a fake accident.*

Jakob realized that he'd left Kellyann alone in the house and, almost bowling over the scarved woman, he sprinted away. As he entered Kellyann's small courtyard, he started yelling for her, and she didn't respond. He ran into the house and up the stairs.

*She isn't in the bathroom. Arrgh!*

When he searched the house and confirmed she was not there, he used WhatsApp to call Bernthaler as he went through her place a second time. Bernthaler answered on the first ring.

"I think they got her," Jakob explained breathlessly. "I'm in Athens at her house in the Plaka. The street's name is Statonos. A fake car crash lured me outside. When I came back, she was gone. It all happened in three minutes."

"Understood," Bernthaler replied. "I will send a team to the house to search for anything."

As Jakob prepared to hang up, he found a small note stuck to the stainless refrigerator with masking tape. In English, it read, "I TOLD YOU NOT TO FUCK WITH ME. UNFREEZE ACCOUNTS,

GIVE ME WHAT YOU TOOK x 3, OR YOU WILL NEVER SEE HER AGAIN." It was written in careful block letters, not something scribbled in a hurry. Jakob described it to Bernthaler, then took a picture of it and sent it to him.

"Is there a safe room?" Bernthaler asked.

*Good question, I hadn't thought of that.*

"I will look, but I don't think so. Don't wait for my response to mobilize your team. Call Hartmann and let him know what's happening. I will call you back if I find her here. In the meantime, check for any civilian or military flights taking off within the next three hours within two hundred kilometers of Athens. Also, check for boat departures."

"They cut the masking tape with scissors. They planned this far in advance. I'm on it," Bernthaler said and hung up.

Jakob looked through her house, estimating the size of rooms to see if a hidden room could exist behind a fake wall. He checked the attic and basement and found no safe room. He was having trouble concentrating.

*They must have been following us. I feel like a part of me has been torn away and I'm bleeding out.*

His balance was off, and he felt faint. He entered the bedroom again, and her scent rushed him. It evoked two opposite reactions. Part of him was on fire and wanted to lie on her bed and scream into the pillow, inhaling her. Part of him turned cold and calculating.

*I will get her back, and Lukashenko will be hurt for this.*

Just before he turned on his laptop, he realized they knew her identity and her location, so they had probably compromised her internet connection and may have had pinhole cameras in the house.

205

Trying to appear casual, he walked through the narrow streets of the ancient Greek city to the fourth closest internet cafe, according to Google Maps. He figured if it were his operation, he'd tap into the closest two internet cafes. In the darkened back area, he took a seat at a desk coated with decades of spilled soda and who knows what else. The entire cafe smelled like a shut-in's laundry basket. He suppressed a shudder, then composed an email.

**Hello my friend. The grumpy White Ruthenian has taken my girlfriend/future wife.**

White Ruthenia is the historic name for Belarus. The Romanians will have figured that out in seconds, but any signal sniffer looking for terms like "Lukashenko" or "Belarus" wouldn't pick it up immediately.

He opened a separate window and created a throwaway Gmail account using a random mix of twenty-six numbers and letters. Then he copied that email address and told his Romanian associate to contact him there, transposed it and emailed it to himself so he could check it later.

**I will double your rate to find out what you can about it/ her in the next 36 hours. I'm looking for pressure points for the W.R. and his country. Also, please tell me as much as possible about the former Leninist who is working with them.**

Jakob assumed they were watching as he got close to her house, and he wanted to appear distraught and scattered. The distraught part didn't take any acting but looking scattered was all acting because he was now hyper-focused. Once at her house, Jakob grabbed two burner phones and went for a walk; after his standard setup, he called his concierge service and requested a private flight to Budapest in four hours and reservations for the next two weeks in Belarus at Minsk's Europe Hotel in the presidential suite. The suite, he said, should be reserved under the name Camille Bougoin.

After trashing the first phone, he next called the man who handled his ground transportation logistics in Europe. An incredibly difficult man to talk to, Jakob used him because he always got the job done.

"Hello," Jakob said, knowing that the man recognized his voice.

"Who the hell is this?" he replied in a time-honored ritual of rudeness.

"I need your help with what may be the oddest thing I've asked of you."

"I hate odd shit," he grumped.

"I want you to buy a hundred and fifty large white trucks and park them at the northern border of Belarus near Russia," Jakob summarized.

"A hundred and fifty trucks? That's insane and exorbitant. What are you, nuts? Used piece-of-shit trucks in Minsk run about 50,000 Euro each, without the trailer. And what's the bullshit about them all being white? You need drivers too?" Jakob had to smile at the man's complete lack of a filter.

"I don't need drivers. And yes, the trucks have to be white, with white cloth-covered trailers. If you can't get enough white ones, paint them white. If you have to buy new ones, buy new ones. It doesn't need to be a good paint job as long as it's quick. If the trailers aren't cloth-covered, cover the hardtops with white cloth." Jakob kept going to get it all out. "And I want it to be done in five days."

"That's impossible, you crazy idiot."

"If you do this, I will pay for the trucks and your fee, and you can keep and re-sell all the trucks and trailers after three weeks," Jakob responded calmly.

"Five days. A hundred and fifty white, soft-covered trucks delivered to the northern border of Belarus near Russia. No drivers. Got it."

*The man is a jerk, but he gets stuff done!*

Before Jakob left for the airport for his Budapest flight, he called the head of his Radioactive Depository Company in Hungary. He was the third person in the world who knew about the gold, and after pleasantries which Jakob found excruciating, knowing that every minute they held Kellyann increased her danger, Jakob told him, "I want to invoke Project Eureka for 120,000 kilograms."

Jakob heard a deep intake of breath on the other end of the line, followed by some rapid-fire keypunching. "Yes sir, we can have fifty percent in thirty-six hours, and the rest in sixty hours. But to clarify, sir, you are asking for a hundred thirty-two imperial tons?"

"That is correct. Are your time estimates assuming 24/7 extraction?" Jakob asked.

"No sir, it was based on standard operating hours. With 24/7, all hands on deck, we should have half in…" he paused and typed rapidly, "in twelve hours and all of it in twenty-four hours."

Jakob knew the mine workers had a significant logistical undertaking ahead of them, during which many of them would not sleep. Normally, he would have felt bad asking people to stay up for twenty-four hours, but Project Eureka ensured everyone involved got paid double time, and the 24/7 extraction doubled that.

"Please upgrade to 24/7. That is perfect, thank you."

Jakob knew that about half of the world's extracted gold was held in jewelry, industrial uses accounted for another 13%, and governments held 17% in reserves. None of those uses resulted in frequent trading, which meant that only about 20% of the world's gold could be traded in the short term. That meant 132 tons of gold hitting the market at once would swing the price massively.

He hung up and turned to tell Kellyann the good news before he caught himself.

*Damn.*

# CHAPTER 34

# LIFE 13.0 -
# HISPANIOLA 2 - 1844

Five months into his micro-lending project, Jakob met with a barefoot farmer who approached him. "*Hola, Señor* Nuevo. My name is Pablo, and I would like a loan of one hundred twenty pesos oro to be paid back in three years at 4.5% interest. I will use the money," he explained, "to irrigate my fields, which should triple my yield. Please."

"What do you grow?" Jakob, as Santiago Nuevo, asked him.

"I grow sugarcane. My soil is rich, and I'm able to get six growths of cane from one planting, but my farm only gets about four months of heavy rain each year. I want to dig a cistern to hold extra water and then release it into my fields to add to the lighter rain I get three months per year."

Jakob's plan was working. Pablo's broker got a bonus.

Jakob saw Pablo again, years later. He approached Jakob, well-dressed and carrying a notebook. He had taught himself reading and mathematics.

Pablo laid out his ambitious plan. "*Hola de nuevo, Señor.* This time I would like a loan of twelve thousand pesos oro to buy the land of my southeastern neighbor who has richer soil and better sun exposure than mine. However, he doesn't irrigate his fields, and he pulls the cane out by the roots each harvest, so he gets no regrowth. His yields are far below mine. I will repay the loan in full in three years at 4.25% interest."

Jakob and Pablo became friends.

Jakob sailed around Hispaniola and the Caribbean islands, doing what good he could, for almost three decades. He set up a similar business on the Tortuga Islands, now known as the Cayman Islands, as he found the people there very enterprising.

While working in the Caribbean, Jakob saw the economies where he lent begin to grow.

While he planted only a few financial seeds, the Dominican Republic and the Tortugas were prospering. Undoubtedly, the social anthropologists of today would feel Jakob's attempts to improve the economies of the islands made them less colorful. But local color doesn't pay for medicine. In Haiti, the average income of a citizen is now one-ninth that of a person in the Dominican Republic. Haitians and Dominicans are on the same island and have identical DNA, but something made a big difference in how their countries turned out. Jakob suspected most of it was because of their different cultural attitudes, and perhaps a small part was due to his efforts. Additionally, the Cayman Islands were doing very well across every measure of wellbeing in the Caribbean, except for obesity. Jakob felt he'd done some good. This partially offset his moral debt from his role in causing religious wars.

When it was time for Santiago Nuevo's next life, he left each of his ten brokers 4% of his estate; 55% he left in the very capable hands of

Pablo, who then started a bank. He added the remaining 5% of the Santiago Nuevo estate to the growing balance of the money that had been compounding since 1625.

# CHAPTER 35

# LIFE 18.0 - BUDAPEST 2021

The day after he left Athens, Jakob entered his office under the small apartment building he'd rented in its entirety in Budapest, surrounded by the People's Park on three sides. There he received an email reply from the Romanians.

Hello my friend, I'm sorry to hear about what happened to Fraulein Weber. We have been working on your requests. Regarding economic leverage points: Belarus owes Russia a payment of €900 million for imported oil and natural gas in five days. They are renegotiating the terms of half of their €42 billion in sovereign debt, and they have payments of €4.4 billion due next week. The largest creditor in this debt facility is Russia.

There are some additional items of interest. Lukashenko's 17-year-old son, Nikolai, is in a relationship with a 14-year-old Polish girl. His older sons are spending the month partying in Ibiza with a great deal of cocaine at the beach house they've rented. Finally, at the urging of his mistress, Lukashenko is going for elective liposculpting surgery where they shape fat to look like a six-pack and getting hair implants in two weeks.

The name of the former FancyBear hacker is Natalia Tchaikovsky. She is exceptionally skilled and a very impressive hacker. She switched her allegiance to Belarus for a onetime payment of €725,000 in gold and double the €46,000 salary she made in Russia.

It took Jakob a while to craft his response to the Romanian team, as he had to create many other documents. Once he completed them, he replied.

Thank you. I'd like you to release the attached document which outlines Lukashenko's plan to roll into Russia and take over a 50km wide strip of land along the borders of Latvia and Estonia that will connect Belarus to the Baltic Sea.

Please release it through Wikileaks. Further, I'd like you to place backdated emails on Lukashenko's server communicating his plans for that operation with other officers in the government. My Russian is passable, but I write Belarusian terribly. Please have someone improve on my word choices so it reads like it came from Lukashenko.

I have also attached the text of the email messages to his department heads. I'd like you to backdate and plant them on their servers, including one to the head of the State Security Committee of the Republic of Belarus, telling him to mass troop transport trucks on the northern

216

border. These should be time-stamped over the last few weeks and marked as read. Please time this so the release to Wikileaks happens in four days.

I want you to create fake orders to the Belarus Army to be sent to the Generals from Lukashenko's email. They should tell the Generals to move the 6th and 11th Brigades of Belarus' mechanized tank divisions to converge on the northern Belarus town of Polotsk, where the 103rd Mobile Brigade is headquartered. This will ostensibly be for "previously unannounced, radio-silent" tank war games among the divisions. The tanks should be there in three days and not travel during the day.

Please reach out to Ms. Tchaikovsky discreetly and offer her €7,500,000 in gold to come work for me for an annual salary of €725,000 per year, with a penthouse condominium on the Fort Lauderdale beach. As a show of good faith, please tell her 141 kg of gold is in the Presidential Suite of the Europe Hotel in Minsk. The gold is in six heavy-duty wheeled suitcases, and we have reserved the room for Camille Bougoin.

Thank you.

Jakob also heard from his Hungarian manager to say that they had completed Project Eureka.

Hello Sir, the Eureka barrels are now in the secure storage facility in Budapest, Hungary, 10 km from your office.

His bank in Budapest was, not surprisingly, Rothschild & Co. But before he could have Rothschild pick up the gold, he had to have the radioactive signage removed.

For that, Jakob called Bernthaler, who assured Jakob he would have a team in the storage facility in six hours, and they would remove and dispose of the outer barrels. When they finished, they would deliver 310 pounds of the gold to the presidential suite of Europe Hotel in Minsk, in six Louis Vuitton wheeled cases.

Jakob did, however, need the Rothschild Bank to do something for him now, so he called his Rothschild private banker and requested that he purchase US $1.2 billion of Belarusian hard currency sovereign bonds over the next three days. It is hard to get a Rothschild private banker to sound flustered, but his request did it.

"One point two billion, with a B, US dollars of Belarus hard currency sovereign bonds?" the banker asked, trying to hide his incredulity.

"Yes."

Jakob could hear rapid typing on a keyboard in the background, before the banker asked, "You recognize that is almost all the liquidity in their hard currency bond market?"

"Yes," Jakob replied again. "That is how I determined the number."

"Very well, sir, we will start today." His voice sounded tentative and still questioning, as if waiting for Jakob to correct him.

"Thank you," Jakob said, cheerfully.

The Belarus bond prices had fallen because Lukashenko had recently rattled international buyers with his ridiculous strong-man tactics. He sent a fighter jet to force down a commercial airplane to a Belarus airport, so he could pull a journalist critical of him off the plane.

218

Jakob then received an email he knew came from Lukashenko's people, despite the vyzrabilipamylku@yahoo.com mail which translated to "You Made a Mistake." In it, they gave Jakob four days to refund three times the money that he and Kellyann donated from his and his son's accounts, and remove the limitation on daily withdrawals, or he would start sending Jakob parts of Kellyann.

Jakob responded quickly.

I recognize a checkmate when I see one. I will triple the money removed from your accounts. You will be able to withdraw funds with no limit by tomorrow morning. Bring her to Vilnius, Lithuania, to the Hotel Vilnia.

Jakob knew this would not be the last demand from Lukashenko, but he needed the man to release Kellyann. Only once he'd freed her could he do what he planned to eliminate Lukashenko's ability to threaten anyone further.

Bernthaler called and let Jakob know that there were no suspicious take-offs near Athens in the ten hours after her abduction. Three boats left the area, but they were all fishing in the Saronic Gulf to the southwest of Athens. Bernthaler had tasked drones to watch them, despite the low probability of Kellyann being on board. Although no suspicious departures had been found, Bernthaler thought it likely that Kellyann had been moved to Belarus. Jakob agreed.

# CHAPTER 36

# LIFE 14.0 - LOUISIANA, USA 1864

After the passing of Santiago Nuevo, Jakob took the name Jacques D'Trous, another play on "two holes," in Louisiana in the Confederate States of America. In early 1864, the US Civil War was ongoing, and Louisiana was a Confederate slave-owning state, with almost fifty percent of its population listed as slaves.

Jakob found slavery a brutal and barbaric system that showed the revolting underbelly of the slave owner. He worked against it in Hungary when the Turks raided the countryside for female slaves, and he worked against it in the heart of the Confederacy.

There were many things that Jakob could not fathom about slavery and, particularly, slavery in America. One that he had never heard articulated was that many of the slaves came from Mali, and areas near it. Yet the richest man in history came from Mali. One hundred years before Jakob Fugger was born, Mansa Musa ruled over the Mali Empire in Africa.

Mansa Musa's fortune made Jakob's look modest. When he took a caravan through Egypt, just the gold gifts to people he met dropped the price of gold by half.

*How could the richest kingdom in the world fall so fast? How could the only export of value to the West be the forced physical labor of the people of Mali? How could Mali not protect itself? How could an uneducated farmer in Louisiana claim ownership of another human? I don't understand it.*

When Jakob arrived as Jacques D'Trous, there was a political concept dubbed "King Cotton" which Louisiana felt would be the secret to winning the war. The King Cotton theory held that if the Confederacy denied the UK access to its cotton, it would force the UK to side with slave owners in the South and protect Confederate ships.

While Jakob found the logic of this concept questionable, he'd seen dumber plans work, and so he undertook to do what he could to undermine King Cotton.

Louisiana did not operate under the same commercial code as the rest of the United States and even the rest of the Confederacy. Their laws were based on French and Spanish civil codes, so he used that to his advantage. Jacques D'Trous purchased controlling interests in almost all the largest insurers of ships in the state. In his new companies, he generated bureaucratic obstacles to insuring those ships that carried the products of slave labor and those engaged in state-sponsored privateering.

Officially, of course, the companies were neutral, but by creating labyrinthine bureaucracies with conflicting layers of objectives, and bonus plans that rewarded managers' compliance with company policies rather than sales, no policies were written. This resulted in hundreds of privateering ships never being launched because out-of-state insurance was so expensive.

One afternoon, an apoplectic boat owner stormed into the insurance office and demanded to see the owner. Jakob agreed to meet with him and invited him into his office. The spartan L-shaped office held Jakob's wooden desk in the center; his chair faced the desk, and Jakob's secretary, facing away from Jakob's desk, silently worked in the smaller alcove.

"What is going on here, you *couyon?*" demanded the man as he charged in. "I have eight privateering ships sitting idle because I can't get a quote for insurance."

Jakob responded, "Is your question rhetorical? It seems as if you answered it yourself."

This aggravated the man further, and he leaned over Jakob's desk. He stood over six feet tall and tried to intimidate Jakob with his size and volume. "You know what I'm asking. Why can't I get a quote for insurance for my damned ships?"

"Oh, but you can get a quote. I'll be happy to give you one now. Let's see, you have eight sailing ships, recently constructed of…oh, constructed of wood…and each carries privateering weapons." Jakob fell silent for a while, then said, "The cost to insure your boats will be ten million per year."

"That's insane. It cost me a fraction of that to build them." The man's eyes went wide, and his face flushed more. Jakob could see a vein on the man's forehead rapidly pulsing.

Jakob responded, "I should hope so, but you see, they made your boats of wood. They're privateering boats, which is a dangerous business, and it turns out wood splinters when hit by cannon balls."

"They make all damned boats of wood, you idiot, and I know wood splinters when hit by cannon balls," the man screamed.

"Well, very good. I'm glad you understand the challenge of insuring your boats. Please have a wonderful day!" Jakob replied as if they had just come to an agreement.

"Why, you son of a… I'm going to kill you!" the man raged, his face now blood red. He raised his walking stick and started to run around Jakob's desk, then slammed directly into Jakob's secretary, who was suddenly standing in his way. Jakob's secretary was an impeccably dressed black man, standing just over seven feet tall and built like the trunk of an oak tree.

In a booming voice, he asked Jakob, "Is there something I can help you with?"

"Let's ask our friend." Jakob turned to the red-faced man, who had lost the color in his face. "Do you, sir, believe we need the help of my secretary?"

"No, we're done here," he sputtered and stormed out, slamming the door hard enough to knock a painting off the wall.

Jakob looked at the fallen painting, then looked at his secretary, who just smiled and started a deep, rumbling laugh. "I got it yesterday. Today it's your turn."

Jakob resignedly stood and re-hung the painting, mumbling, "But you were standing right next to it." Then he too started laughing.

It is unclear how much of a difference Jakob made, but a year after his purchases, Louisiana had surrendered, slaves were freed, and soon after that, the state was readmitted to the Union. The state's King Cotton plan was a horrible failure...for the state.

Jakob revamped his companies' underwriting rules and bonus plans at that point, allowing them to write insurance very profitably for a vast number of ships and businesses going forward.

After a decade in New Orleans, Jakob traveled up the Mississippi and tried to do good where he could.

# CHAPTER 37

# LIFE 18.0 -
# SOUNDING BOARD 2021

It had been three days since Kellyann's kidnapping. Jakob slept four hours a night only through sheer force of will, but he couldn't shake the concern that he'd missed something. He knew Hartmann was feeling helpless, so Jakob WhatsApp'd him to use him as a sounding board.

"Hello, sir," Hartmann picked up on the second ring.

"Hi. You are, or were, a lawyer before you got into this business, weren't you?"

"Um, yes, I am still a lawyer," he replied. This was the first time Hartmann ever sounded surprised by something Jakob had asked him. "Is that important?"

"I'd like to hire you as my lawyer and invoke the attorney-client privilege," Jakob explained, "then I want to lay out my plans and have you double-check my logic."

"Ah, okay, now I understand. Yes, please Venmo me one dollar as a retainer, and then we can talk. My Venmo account is @ Hartman6969. Before you ask, the system assigned it," he responded, clearly embarrassed.

Once he transferred the money, Jakob began, "I don't trust that this is the last we'll hear from Lukashenko. Any rendezvous agreement will involve treachery on his part. I will transfer the money he wants, but the moment we can get Kellyann and we verify that they haven't implanted a tracker, I need to render him harmless. To do that, I'm hitting him on several fronts.

"I've bought as many of the Belarus bonds as I can, for just over one billion dollars, and I'll start dumping them soon to flood the market and tank the price."

"How will that defang him?" asked Hartmann.

"Belarus has two huge payments due to Russia, and the bond sales will make his currency plummet compared to the Russian ruble, so he'll have to scramble to get cash. Simultaneously, I will dump gold on the market, dropping the price. This will cut off his ability to sell gold reserves to raise hard cash, or to borrow against the gold. The goal of this is to force him to call Putin and ask for more time on the payments. I want to keep him distracted from exacting revenge.

"I have hired his best hacker, and she is working with our Romanians to plant emails that show Lukashenko is planning a small invasion into Russia's western territory to give him a land bridge to the Baltic Sea and access to a wet port. I have one hundred fifty cloth-covered, white trucks parked, visible to satellites, along the border…"

"A hundred and fifty white unmarked trucks?" Hartmann interrupted, "like the ones Putin used to invade Crimea in Ukraine?"

"Coincidentally, these are identical to those," Jakob responded. "Breadcrumb trails to the planted emails will be pushed to Russia's current FancyBear hackers, so Putin will quickly know about them.

Further, unbeknownst to Lukashenko, he has ordered two-thirds of his tanks to the northern border for surprise maneuvers."

Hartmann whistled. "Remind me not to piss you off. Putin is going to eliminate Lukashenko if he thinks Belarus will stiff him on debt payments and make a grab for a piece of Russia. He might even take over Belarus. What about Lukashenko's successors?"

"Right," Jakob replied, "Lukashenko doesn't trust his two oldest sons, for good reason. I hate to agree with his judgment, but they are idiots. He's been grooming his youngest son to take over after him. Unfortunately for them both, his 17-year-old son is having sex with an underage girl and is about to get publicly arrested for it in Poland. His older sons are partying with pyramids of cocaine in Ibiza and both the Spanish *Cuerpo Nacional de Policía*, and TMZ will be tipped off about the house party.

"As for Putin taking over Belarus, I'm doing what I can to support spontaneous protests for Sviatlana Tsikhanouskaya to be given control of the country. Aside from protesters, there may be large groups of onlookers that somehow get in the way of any police attempts to arrest the protesters. It is interesting how far $1,000 can go in a country where the average worker earns less than US $700 per month. I wouldn't be surprised if an anonymous party lends Tsikhanouskaya's fledgling government funds to acquire several portable versions of Israel's Iron Dome missile defense system. The red tape that prevented Lukashenko's government from buying a shopping list of western military hardware will disappear when Tsikhanouskaya takes control. And I'm confident she will have no problem getting loans to pay for it all, as I will guarantee the loans."

Hartmann replied, "It seems only fair, given that she won the election in 2020. Okay, what about the files they have on you? What will prevent the next ruler from trying the same thing?"

"Good question!" Jakob paused, then replied, "I have had his hacker, now on our payroll, make corruptive changes to the addresses, account numbers, and personal information in their files. While it will look nearly the same, the information will be gibberish. She has also set up a virus to corrupt the backups."

"Smart," Hartmann replied. "What if they don't release Kellyann?"

Jakob's internal temperature dropped. "If he hurts, or docsn't release, Kellyann, he will really piss me off and these plans will seem mild compared to what I will unleash on him."

"How will you get Kellyann away from the exchange?"

"I have arranged for the Lithuanian military to give Kellyann, me, and our hacker a ride in their AS365 Dauphin helicopter, escorted by two of their Mi-17 helicopters, from Vilnius to Stockholm. They're interested in refinancing the four Blackhawk helicopters they bought in 2020, and this is a courtesy ride as far as they're concerned."

"Yes, sir. I think your plan is solid, but as your new lawyer, I should remind you not to do anything that is against the law." That broke the tense mood.

Jakob smiled when he replied, "Of course. Thank you, counselor."

They then spent several hours fine-tuning the details of the plan and adding some additional ideas.

# CHAPTER 38

# LIFE 16.0 -
# GIRLS' EDUCATION 1950

The safety, comfort, and availability of commercial air travel over long distances made Jakob's life much easier. In 1950, he could leave Europe and be in America, not in the seven weeks it took in the eighteenth century, but in a matter of hours.

Consequently, Jakob spent a great deal of time in North America, and it was in the late 1940s that he determined he should work to help women there. He hadn't been able to help them much in his earlier lives, but women in the USA were making significant strides in improving their lot in life.

Real and obstructive gender-based discrimination against women still existed, but it was getting worn away every year. After studying the issue, he felt there were two things that were slowing their march for equality that he might impact. First, the fact that only women got pregnant worked against their achieving economic parity with men. Although more women were graduating from high school, far fewer women were earning college degrees than men.

Donating funds to formal or structured charities had not resulted in the changes that Jakob wanted. More frequently than not, the charity grew but the problem didn't diminish. He also found that throwing money at a problem had mixed results and that the outcome he had hoped for was rarely the outcome that emerged.

One way Jakob thought he could be productive was to work upstream, focusing on supporting people, organizations, or grassroots movements that could influence change along the lines he wanted.

After digging deep, Jakob felt women lagged in getting advanced education, not because they weren't intelligent enough, but primarily because of the perceptions of women's roles in society. Although women had taken on "men's jobs" during World War II, there were lingering perceptions about what women could and should do. These were codified in the educational system that provided a "differentiated curriculum" for girls in high schools. That, he felt, could go away. He further believed that if he could find and fund a way to make it easier for women to pursue degrees and combine that with programs to make more women want to get college degrees, it might work.

Although he could see where women's education was, and he knew where women's education could be, he had to admit that he didn't know what to do to change things. So, he tried a version of what he had done in the Dominican Republic.

To support the objectives, Jakob had to suppress his latent discomfort around women and start talking to them. Much to his surprise, he enjoyed it. He traveled the nation and met in small groups with professors and concerned women who'd graduated college. First, he set up a foundation, which he whimsically called the Dragonwyke Group. He then secured office space in San Francisco and hired a whip-smart woman to help him identify how he could best put the money to work. Dragonwyke raised several million dollars from "anonymous donors," and he began visiting women's groups and individual women that his associate had identified. The amounts he parceled out seemed small to him, but as the groups he met with were volunteers, it had an outsized effect.

Some women he met wanted to fix every social ill, which made him wary of their focus, but he met a few that were determined to get more girls to attend colleges. He invested more with them. One in particular was an attractive woman in her sixties with gray hair and intense eyes.

"What is your aim?" she asked him when they sat down in her office stacked with books and smelling like clove cigarettes.

"I want to give women more control over their lives. Specifically, I want to increase the rate at which young women pursue degrees until they equal or surpass the rate of men doing the same."

"Ooh, I like you. You didn't use any academic catchphrases."

Jakob responded, "I don't know any academic catchphrases, so that had something to do with it."

She nodded, "Fair point. Where would you start?"

"To answer your question, I don't know. I've already donated to a dozen small groups of women who want to boost female enrollment. I think I'll just keep up with that."

"How do you track their results?" she asked.

"I don't track them. I trust them."

"Ohh, I really like you. How much are we talking about?"

Jakob replied, "Eighty thousand is the average of what I've donated to each so far."

"Ho-lee sheet. That's twenty times my annual salary. I expected you to say two thousand. We could do a lot with eighty thousand dollars."

"Very well, here's eighty thousand dollars." Handing her what looked like a brown lunch bag, he said, "Go for it."

Jakob planted seed money with anyone he met he thought might work hard to improve the educational prospects for women. Though he'd tried to invest far more, over a decade he'd funded just over eight million dollars in roughly one hundred small groups. He knew that many of the groups disbanded through inertia or frustration, but some kept working, and he could see slow changes taking place.

Pregnancy management, as he thought of it, proved a more challenging issue for Jakob to address.

The Vatican had declared that any non-natural form of birth control was a sin, and Jakob considered himself a Catholic. He felt that while the Church wanted more Catholic babies, it wasn't as concerned with the burden that many babies placed on both Catholic families and eventually the Catholic babies themselves.

In many families, he discovered a mindset about having children that carried over from medieval times—have lots of kids so some of them take care of you when you're old. Despite the plunging death rate in children, and social programs to supplement the elderly, women still had large families and spent much of their lives pregnant, nursing, raising kids, and helping with homework.

If a mother raised a child on her own, particularly in the 1950s, in most cases, she committed herself and her child to a life of poverty. The same was not true of fathers who walked away from women they'd impregnated. A man could move and avoid the shame, or claim the girl, whom he had recently convinced of his undying love, was easy and the baby could be from one of many fathers.

Further, if couples had children too early, or if they had enormous families, they increased their probability of poverty. And, if a child was unwanted, it was tragic all around.

Jakob had firsthand experience with popes reconsidering the definition of a sin, so he dedicated significant time and money to get the Vatican to refine its position on birth control. Through intermediaries, he built agreement at the highest levels of the Church and in the powerful papal commission that non-traditional birth control, meaning anything but abstinence, would not be a sin.

Jakob knew, however, that while governments move glacially, the Vatican barely moved at all.

He focused not only on the Church. Through many anonymous grants, he supported the Malthusian League and the activist Margaret Sanger to overcome the Comstock laws, which made it illegal to talk about birth control. He also funded research into the hormonal regulation of fertility, which resulted in Enovid or "the pill."

In Europe and Asia, in the 1950s, the pill gave women some control over their future if they had sex. In the USA, The Federal Drug Administration moved with Vatican-like slowness, but, after a ridiculously expensive lobbying effort, determined it could be prescribed.

After the FDA approval, the Vatican was due to give its blessing to birth control, but despite his extensive network of informants guaranteeing Jakob his desired outcome, someone got to Pope Paul VI just before the announcement. To almost everyone's amazement, Paul VI announced that birth control was "inherently wrong."

This came as a complete surprise to Jakob. His efforts to sway Paul VI had failed entirely, one of his most expensive failures ever.

He worried that the pope's proclamation would derail the progress that had been made, but over time, he saw women and couples taking greater control of their lives and family sizes adjusted.

Seventy years later, as he looked back, he wondered if the compounding effect of educated women having educated daughters might have gone a bit too far. Women were enrolling in and graduating from college in far greater numbers than men. Women comprised almost 60% of higher education students, and although women were not paid at parity with men, Jakob had little doubt that would be remedied sooner rather than later.

To a large degree, he found that women now had far greater control over when, where, and with whom they would get pregnant. Men were being left behind by independent, well-educated women. Over time, he figured the pendulum would swing back and gender would no longer be a factor in whether a person attained their goals.

# CHAPTER 39

# LIFE 18.0 -
# FADE TO GRAY 2021

They crammed the van with equipment, Jakob, Bernthaler, and their newest hire, Natalia Tchaikovsky. The former FancyBear hacker did not look at all like what Jakob expected. He had clearly seen too much television, because he'd expected her to be a slender 20-year-old with purple hair and multiple piercings. However, Natalia looked like, and was, a grandmother.

When she sat in front of a computer, however, she became a machine. Jakob had transferred the funds back into Lukashenko's accounts and anxiously awaited the time to pick up Kellyann in Lithuania, as agreed.

Jakob had never mounted an operation like the one underway, with a dozen former special operators on the roofs of buildings surrounding the Hotel Vilnia. Four pairs were staying as guests in the hotel itself, and Jakob had Bernthaler managing a fleet of drones watching the surrounding area.

The three helicopters sat ready for immediate departure from a park near the beautiful *Baltasis Tiltas* bridge where it crossed the *Neris* River.

Bernthaler broke the silence of the van as he spoke into his headset, "Two vans and a truck on the move, on the E28, just inside the Belarus border, moving fast towards Vilnius."

That gave them about half an hour if Kellyann was in one of the vans. They had to be prepared for multiple decoys.

"Chatter is picking up," said Natalia in perfectly accented English, "all encrypted...yes, it's encrypted but in 16-bit, such amateur *pridurki*." Her fingers flew over the three keyboards in front of her, and soon through the van's speakers they could hear radio exchanges in Belarusian. Jakob turned to give her a thumbs up, but she already had a finger in the air and a moment later, on his screen, text appeared with near real-time translation into English.

"Whoa!" Bernthaler and Jakob blurted at the same time, as they shared a look that conveyed their "Holy shit!" thoughts.

"Sir," Bernthaler said after a minute, "there is activity at the border." Jakob pulled up the drone views and could see vehicles fanning out at the border.

The hacker interrupted. "The vans on the highway are a decoy. She's at the border. They're trying to set you up and trick you into entering Belarus. Lukashenko is such a predictable dick." She flew through screens of Cyrillic text.

"Let's go to the border. Alert the choppers," Jakob told Bernthaler, then Whatsapp'd Hartmann as the van started up and they sped to the border. He had a plan for this possibility and hoped Lukashenko's men would stay true to form.

When the group arrived at the border, they realized it was a mess. Two days of rain resulted in mud everywhere. On the Lithuanian side, thirty feet inside the border, a massive, ultra-industrial dump truck, the size of a house with tires as tall as a man, was starting and stopping, loudly grinding through gears and stalling. The noise made it hard to concentrate. On the truck, the driver was yelling at a mechanic, who was banging on round gauges on the front to no effect. The noise of the engine trying to start made talking impossible.

The Belarus border police had closed down the actual crossing point. There was an armored car parked with just the front of the car over the white line signifying the border, but the wheels were still in Belarus. Jakob could see Kellyann in the passenger seat behind the bulletproof glass.

*She is alive! Yes!*

He gave her an exaggerated wink and saw her burst into laughter.

The Belarus army had three amphibious, armored scout cars which looked like flattened Humvees. Surrounding the scout cars were thirty soldiers standing in a semicircle. Each of the soldiers was carrying a machine gun. They were relaxed because they weren't facing much firepower.

Jakob's side was significantly outgunned. The commercial van with Bernthaler, Natalia, and Jakob inside idled just behind two lightly armored Toyota Hiluxes. Together, they were no match for even one of the armored scout cars.

From inside the van, Jakob activated a loudspeaker and said in Belarusian, "We transferred back three times what we took. We did what you asked. Now, give her back."

"Come and get her. You will have safe passage," was the response.

Jakob expected they would try to get him over the border. If he crossed into Belarus, he knew they would arrest him and Kellyann.

"That is not what we agreed!" Jakob replied, sounding defeated.

"Do you want this girl or not?" the Belarus captain taunted.

Jakob clicked the radio three times in quick succession, and his plan unfolded at high speed.

As the door to the van opened as if Jakob were getting out, the captain on the Belarus side stepped out of the armored car, using the open door as protection. The instant that happened, another man appeared over the top lip of the dump truck and fired a stainless-steel harpoon, trailing thick metal wire, at the armored car. It hit just above the front bumper, sinking in several inches, then clicking open with a burst of sparks. Inside the armored car, Jakob saw Kellyann's eyes go wide. The seemingly disabled massive truck's engine roared to life and reversed, dragging the harpooned armored car over the Lithuanian border as if it were a child's toy, leaving the captain unprotected, so he dove for cover.

The entire process took no more than five seconds; the surprised Belarusian soldiers hit the ground and focused their machine guns on the dump truck. Nobody fired because none of them wanted to be first to fire across an international border into a NATO country without specific orders. If they weren't shot or jailed, the paperwork they'd have to complete for having started an international incident would be crushing.

The massive size and the roar of the dump truck engine allowed the choppers to get close without being seen. Seconds later, emerging from behind the dump truck, they swooped into an arc on Jakob's side, each of the three helicopters bristling with eight shiny gray missiles pointed at the troops. They hovered menacingly.

All Belarusian eyes were on the choppers, given their sudden appearance and the firepower they brought. By that point, the dump truck had dragged the armored car twenty feet into Lithuania, but Kellyann was not yet safe.

The Toyotas moved to block the armored car from any gunfire as Jakob jumped out of the van, ran crouched over to the armored car and pulled Kellyann into his arms. From the muddy wheat fields on either side of the road, sixteen mercenaries in grass ghillie suits over heavy bulletproof vests raced towards them, looking like fast-moving hay piles with big guns.

They surrounded Jakob and Kellyann, then as a group, they jogged further into Lithuania as the middle chopper descended behind the dump truck to land. When they reached it, Hartmann helped them climb aboard. With nimbleness belying her age, Natalia jumped from the reversing van and climbed into the chopper. Hartmann pulled her aboard before turning and speeding off, flying low over the ground.

After kissing Kellyann for far too short a time, Jakob strapped in, and they pulled on the headsets that would allow them all to hear each other.

"That was amazing!" was the first thing Jakob heard Kellyann say when he got the headset on. She was smiling. "Who brings machine guns to an attack helicopter fight? Silly Belarusians!"

Everyone was laughing as Jakob said, "Good to see you again, my love, but these aren't actually attack helicopters. Lithuania wouldn't allow us to start a war."

"But the missiles?" both Natalia and Kellyann asked simultaneously.

Hartmann reached beside his seat and pulled out a missile and tossed it to a startled Kellyann. She caught it and started laughing. "Plastic? I…it's…plastic," she couldn't complete her sentence.

She was laughing too hard as she hit Jakob with the air-to-ground missile.

"PVC, glue, and spray paint, and we had very scary missiles," responded Jakob, finally trapping her missile under his arm. "Kellyann, I'd like to introduce you to our newest security employee, Natalia Tchaikovsky, the world's best hacker, and to Hartmann, the head of my US security team."

"Thank you both!" She reached over and held Natalia's hand and waved at Hartmann.

Natalia gently patted Kellyann's hand in full grandmother mode as they flew over the Lithuanian countryside. "It was my pleasure. I'm so sorry that awful man kidnapped you."

Natalia then turned to Jakob, back in full hacker mode, holding up a slim Apple Airbook. "One, all of Lukashenko's accounts are empty except for the $1.5 million he officially reports as his net worth.

"Two, my former colleagues at FancyBear received the leaked emails about Lukashenko's plans to take a Russian corridor to the sea yesterday. They informed Putin this morning at 5:30 a.m.

"Three, the KGB has been tipped off about the tanks and white troop transport vehicles massing at the northern border of Belarus. Satellites were re-tasked four hours ago, and now the Russian army is mobilizing twenty-four battalions to their southern border with Belarus.

"Four, your bulk sale of gold dropped the spot price by $715 per ounce at the close last night. Fortunately, I sold my gold at US $1,825 per ounce two days ago."

"Fortunately, indeed. Thank you," Jakob replied, knowing full well she'd hacked his email where she learned about his pending gold sales.

Hartmann then took over the briefing. "Belarus bonds are selling for forty-two cents on the dollar. Between that and the crashing price of gold, Lukashenko can't make the payments to Russia. He reached out fifty minutes ago to Putin to ask for more time. It was apparently not a comfortable conversation."

Kellyann looked over at Natalia, who shook her head with a little chortle. "A very uncomfortable conversation for Lukashenko."

Jakob knew she had somehow listened in.

Hartmann continued, "*The Cuerpo Nacional de Policía* were tipped off about Lukashenko's older sons' cocaine-fueled parties in Ibiza, and TMZ received HD-quality drone video of the Lukashenko boys both selling and snorting coke. They will be raided within the next fifteen minutes. All exits have been blocked from the house they rented, and both speedboats have been disabled. The police are armed with detailed legal briefs which confirm that the brothers do not have diplomatic immunity.

"Two hours ago, the Polish police stormed a hotel suite where they found Nikolai Lukashenko in bed with his underage girl-friend. He is being held in jail where his wounds are being treated. The Polish police are not very gentle with child sex offenders, par-ticularly those that unsuccessfully try to hide behind diplomatic immunity.

"Finally, today started four days of spontaneous, but well-funded, protests in Belarus' largest cities to support Sviatlana Tsikhanouskaya, who most believe won the last election."

There was silence over the headphones for about ten seconds be-fore Kellyann looked over at Jakob, smiling, and said, "I really love you!"

As the helicopters sped into the gray mist that covered the countryside, she kissed him again. Natalia and Hartmann, who had seen everything in their lives, had to look away, embarrassed because of the intensity of the kiss.

# CHAPTER 40

# LIFE 18.0 -
# DING DONG 2021

From the front page of the Belarusian Наша Ніва newspaper three days later:

English Translation

LUKASHENKO DEAD

We report the death of a great patriot and our long-standing President, Alexander Lukashenko. He died while under anesthesia for an unspecified medical procedure.

One unnamed top-ranking Belarusian official speculates perhaps it is best that he died when he did because two of his sons were arrested for selling cocaine in Spain and his youngest son, believed to be his eventual successor, was arrested for the rape of a minor in Poland.

Today had been declared by Belarus' Head of Administration, Igor Sergeyenko, as a "day of mourning," but spontaneous street celebrations have taken it over with the repeated chants in English, "Ding dong, the bitch is dead."

Restaurants, grocers and bars in towns throughout the republic have opened their doors and are giving away free beer and vodka. Traffic has come to a standstill as people leave their cars and dance in the streets.

The Supreme Court of the Republic of Belarus moved quickly to replace Lukashenko with Sviatlana Tsikhanouskaya, after a top election official announced she was, in fact, elected President of Belarus, and because of a small "scrivener's error" it has been earlier reported that it was Lukashenko who'd won.

.

# A NOTE ON HISTORICAL ACCURACY

Jakob Fugger – Jakob Fugger was a real person. He became one of the richest men in the world with his fortune estimated to have been equivalent to $400 billion (with a "B") in 2021 dollars. Every attempt was made to present him accurately, given that his longevity is fiction.

Vladimir Putin – Officially, his net worth is $150,000, and though there is evidence of the Oligarch Squeeze, he denies it. Every attempt was made to present the rise of the oligarchs and FancyBear accurately. Officially, all claims in this book about Putin are fiction.

Alexander Lukashenko – Like Putin, much about him has been confirmed by many sources, but he denies it. Officially, his net worth is $1,500,000. Officially, all claims in this book about Lukashenko and his sons are fiction.

Mayer Rothschild – The financial and social success of Mayer and his sons is accurate. His choking death and replacement with Jakob are fiction.

Dutch Tulip Bubble – Exotic tulips did become so coveted they sold for the price of a house until they crashed and returned to the more normal price of a sandwich.

Indulgences – Every attempt was made to present them accurately. Popes, Kings and Emperors – Every attempt was made to present them accurately.

Blackfeet Reservation – Jakob Fugger's involvement with the Native American casinos is fiction. Every attempt was made to present tribal law accurately.

Girls' Education – Jakob Fugger's involvement is fiction, although women's academic enrollment dominance is accurate.

Dominican Republic – Jakob Fugger's involvement is fiction.
Insuring Confederate Ships – Jakob Fugger's involvement is fiction.

Made in United States
North Haven, CT
20 June 2022

20421593R00141